To dear Melissa,

Some tales to amuse
you during your few
moments for relaxing.

A very happy birthday
for n° 20!

Lots of love,

Mom

4/15/86

WHEN IN
FLORENCE

WHEN IN FLORENCE

Richard Cortez Day

DOUBLEDAY & COMPANY, INC.
GARDEN CITY, NEW YORK
1986

Library of Congress Cataloging in Publication Data
Day, Richard Cortez, 1927–
    When in Florence.
    I. Title.
PS3554.A9657W47   1986   813′.54
ISBN 0-385-23157-1
Library of Congress Catalog Card Number 85–10171

This book is for Janyce

Contents

O insensata cura de' mortali,
   quanto son difettivi silogismi
   quei che ti fanno in basso batter l'ali!
Chi dietro a iura e chi ad amforismi
   sen giva, e chi seguendo sacerdozio,
   e chi regnar per forza o per sofismi,
e chi rubare e chi civil negozio,
   chi nel diletto de la carne involto
   s'affaticava e chi si dava a l'ozio,
quando, da tutte queste cose sciolto,
   con Bëatrice m'era suso in cielo
   cotanto glorïosamente accolto.
             —Dante, *Paradiso*

O senseless care of mortals! How faulty the reasonings that make you fly downward! One was pursuing the law, another worldly maxims, one chasing the priesthood, one seeking to rule by force or guile, another by robbery, and another by civil business. While one rolled wearily in the pleasures of the flesh, and another gave himself over to sloth, I was with Beatrice, high in heaven, gloriously received!

WHEN IN FLORENCE

A Chagall Story

One afternoon in Via della Spada, Guido Iannotti's chest knocked him over. He had been knocked over by lots of things in his long life. He remembered particularly a certain brown horse with a mean eye and a mule's trick of kicking sideways. Mamma, he almost hadn't gotten up that time. But never before had his own chest knocked him down.

As he lay there on the street, he saw faces bending over him—Paolo the greengrocer from around the corner, Fulvia from the bakery—and farther back a circle of others, acquaintances from the quarter, passersby, a tourist or two. How serious they all were! Fulvia, with both hands to her cheeks, said, *"È morto?"* and Paolo replied, *"Morto, sì."*

Dead? Guido Iannotti dead? If they would give him a few minutes, let him rest a little, he would scramble to his feet and do a dance. But as he saw himself there on the stones, mouth open, gulping like a fish, he had to admit that they might have a point. The sickly gray color of his face, the caved-in cheeks: even at eighty a man should look better than that. Perhaps if someone would straighten his hat . . .

An ambulance nosed into the narrow street, siren howling, and the crowd parted respectfully. But it kept right on going. Guido rose to follow it with his eyes. *Madonna Santa,* it was on another mission! He looked down and saw a second ambulance, this one silent, stopping beside the form on the sidewalk. Two men got out, in no rush at all. They lifted him as if he weighed no more than a picture of himself. "Hey, easy—watch my hat!" he said.

One of the men picked up his hat and tossed it in after him. Guido dove for a look. He saw his shoe soles, like the letter *V,* and, within the *V,* the yellow flower in his buttonhole and the bottom of the jaw he'd been shaving for more than sixty years. The men closed the doors. They got in and drove away. Guido watched. No, they weren't heading for the hospital.

Fulvia, with flour on her cheeks, crossed herself. The passersby moved on. Paolo went back into his shop, where a customer was testing the pears. "Hey, signora," he said, "buy first, then squeeze!" Within a few minutes, life was back to normal in Via della Spada. Guido was gone and forgotten.

"So, I'm a spirit," he said. "So this is what it's like." He knocked a ripe pear onto the floor right under Paolo's nose. Paolo squinted and scratched his head. *"Aou,* I'm invisible," Guido said. He rolled three tomatoes out of the box, knocked another pear to the floor, and flung a bunch of grapes at Paolo's feet. Paolo was the kind who hid inferior fruit under the good ones, who short-changed you unless you counted every lira, who weighed his hand with the vegetables. Guido had bought that hand a thousand times. He turned the cashbox upside down and let the bills flutter. Paolo rolled his eyes, crossed himself, howled like a dog.

This was sport. This was revenge. How he'd longed to get even with that tyrant Paolo. He felt better than he'd felt for a long while. Where was the old ache in his hip? They must have carted it off in the ambulance. He felt like getting out and doing things. But since he wasn't sure how much time he had before going to heaven, he thought he should get home and put his affairs in order. He had always made duty his first priority. He didn't want to leave a mess for his daughter—it wouldn't be right.

In Via del Moro, how often he'd cursed the darkness. It wasn't a street, it was a slit between rows of houses. It might have been fine for an astronomer—you could set your clock by the flash the sun made as it passed over—but for the people who had to live there, well, he was surprised they weren't as blind as moles. What did they need eyes for? They got where they were going by touching the walls.

The stairway to his apartment had been his cross to bear. Eight flights, eighty-eight steps, and with what reward at the top? A cramped dungeon of a place, a kind of subcellar, as if they'd built the house upside down. He and his wife had raised three children there, the whole family pale as mushrooms, and then their daughter, Lisa, and her husband had moved in and raised their two, and now one of those two had come back with *her* husband, to raise yet more children in the gloom. There had always been plenty of children. Laura, bless her, had died ten years ago because of her weight. To climb the stairs, she'd had to work twice as hard as Guido. Finally, her heart gave out.

This time, he skipped up the steps and wasn't even winded. In the apartment he saw that the family had already heard. News travels fast in the Santa Maria Novella quarter; Lisa was already wearing black. But what was this? Her husband, Marco, who was too lazy to work and get an apartment of his own, was going through the dresser, throwing Guido's things out, putting his own clothes in the drawers. And look, there on the bed, all his personal belongings—his letters, the pictures he'd saved, Laura's wedding ring, his documents, his keys, his pocketknife, his own wedding ring! Lisa and Marco were going through everything, moving into his room, and him not even decently buried yet. Look at them, stretching out on the bed, bouncing, testing it! His own family, the ungrateful wretches!

But then a thought crossed his mind. Could there have been a funeral already, and he'd missed it? Perhaps they'd put him in the ground with proper ceremonies and tears, with the jonquil in his buttonhole, with his hat resting on his chest. While he'd been kicking fruit around Paolo's shop, perhaps the funeral had come and gone. In this spirit life, he could see, he was still a puppy. He had a lot to learn. Where, for example, did one catch the bus for heaven? Shouldn't there be an angel picking him up about now, or at least a notice pinned up somewhere?

He left his family to their predictable concerns. Life was for the living, and he wanted no part of it. Let Lisa and her husband have the sagging bed, the old backbreaker; let them go on dragging their bodies up the stairs. That was life? All that labor? And for what? Free as a bird, he took a few turns around Piazza Santa Maria Novella, keeping an eye out for the angel. On a cornice of the church, he sat next to a pigeon. Down below, two priests strolled in the April sunshine. There were young lovers, hurrying businessmen, gawking tourists. He dove from the ledge, swooped low, and like a lark fired up and over the buildings to the train station. Perhaps it wouldn't be a bus, but one of those trains, a funicular, like he'd ridden on his honeymoon at Vesuvius.

But there was nothing at the station, either. If he could find some other spirits . . . Where in Florence would spirits hang out? He sailed over the Arno and tried Santa Maria del Carmine, then Santo Spirito. Nothing doing. He swung back across the river to the big cathedral, the Duomo, and alighted on the main altar. There was a mass in progress. To get some attention, he hovered right over the priest's head, then blew out one of the candles, but the priest went right on with his sermon. Guido fanned his notes onto the floor, but he kept talking, the old fool. All is vanity, remember that you too will die, and so forth. The idiot. Guido, with exquisite pleasure, spiraled up into the dome, then plunged and did hair-raising turns at floor level around the rows of columns. Then he shot from the church right through a ten-foot-thick stone wall. He didn't get a scratch.

At Santa Croce and San Miniato al Monte, he fared no better than at the other churches. Nothing but people, no angels, no other spirits. Had he missed the helicopter? Where was the elevator? He drifted into All Saints' for a look around, and there, in the right transept, in a glass case, he saw the *corpo incorrotto,* the uncorrupted remains, of Saint Giacomo Melanzane, who had been archbishop of Florence from A.D. 1389 until 1439.

The body wasn't exactly fresh, but it was still recognizable as a man's, though the face was shrunken, leathery, and brown, and the miter had tipped a bit forward on the brow. But there were the eyes, the nose, and the down-turned, sour-looking mouth. In fact, the saint, in Guido's estimation, looked pretty much like he himself would have looked with a few hundred more years on him.

But miracle of miracles! The eyes opened a little and looked sideways. With the smallest of gestures, but unmistakable in meaning, the head moved: come here.

"In there?" Guido said.

The saint nodded. With some distaste, Guido went through the glass.

It wasn't too bad. The see-through coffin, though not large, contained the two of them easily, and there was only a faint dusty smell, like very dry leaves. He said, "Thank you, Your Reverence. I was beginning to think I was alone in the universe."

"You are. And call me Giacco. It's good of you to call. I haven't had a decent conversation in God knows how long. It's too bad we can't have coffee. That's the one thing I miss most. I like it strong, black, sweet—almost syrup. It puts hair on your chest. Remember the taste? Remember how the first swallow goes straight to your brain?"

"Yes, I remember," Guido said. "But what I want to know is, how do I get to heaven? I seem to be stuck here, between two worlds. I must have missed something."

"Heaven? Ha, there isn't any."

"There isn't? Just hell, then? I thought . . ."

"No hell, either. I don't know where those notions come from —it was long before my time. Anyway, they're false."

"But there must be an afterlife. Look, we're talking, and we're both dead."

"We're that, all right. Look at me. Would you believe I used to be over six feet tall? You're lucky—they plopped you right in the ground. They tanned me like a horsehide and left me to be stared at. It's humiliating. The loathing, the disgust on people's faces— it's like being a leper. Everyone turns away."

"But you're Saint Melanzane. I thought saints were enthroned in splendor, close to God."

"You've been in the Baptistery, I see. Idiot artists! What thrones? What God? Anyway, where would you set up a throne? It's just air up there. It's less than air. What would you stand a throne on?"

"Then this is all there is?"

"It could be worse. Cheer up. Have you tried hovering and swooping? Sailing's a lot of fun. You can go through walls, you know, and play tricks on people."

"I've done all that. It's—forgive me—kind of boring, isn't it? Where are all the other spirits? There must be millions of us, somewhere."

"You're new at this. You've got to stop thinking of where and when, for there aren't any. Millions, you say? Billions—quadrillions. They're out in the universe, mostly. You almost never meet one. No, this is it—you're on your own. Do what you can with what you've got."

"But, Your Reverence—"

"Stop that. Do I look like a thing to be revered?"

"Well then, Giacco. The universe—you admit there is one. But you say there's no God. So where did the universe come from?"

"Oy, one of those. Just my luck. I never see anyone, and when someone comes along, he turns out to be a philosopher! Sludge, that's where it came from. A big gob of sludge."

"Then who created the sludge?"

"How do I know? It created itself, then diversified. It turned itself into sun and moon, trees, birds, bugs, and people, not to mention lions and lambs. It's all sludge, when you break it down."

"The soul?"

"Sludge."

"Christ? Mary? The Apostles?"

"Yep. Say, there's a nun in a box over at Santissima Annunziata. Saint Ambrosia, I think her name is. Why don't you coast over and have a chat with her? She might like some company. If I remember right, she was a real student of these questions. Augustine, Jerome, Aquinas—they were her boys. Pop over there, she's a laugh a minute, or used to be."

"All right, I'll go see her," Guido said. "But is this all you do, lie here and grump, until you get another body to inhabit?"

"Get another body? Does that happen?"

"I don't know, Giacco—you're the archbishop. I've heard of it, that's all I can say. It's called reincarnation."

"Wouldn't you know? As if once wasn't enough. Twice yet. But maybe it won't happen. I've never heard of it. Can we choose a body, do you think, or do we take potluck? What if it was a cow or pig? Or a toad? What if it was a woman? Imagine that!"

"Maybe it won't happen," Guido said. "Don't be upset. I'm sorry I brought it up."

"Another body, Jesus." He fell silent for a few moments. Then he brightened. "Say, would you like to go out for a while, hover some? We could shoot down to Rome. The Vatican's nice—very well kept up. Or we could swing down around Africa—"

"No thanks," Guido said. "I want to find my wife if I can. Her name is Laura—gray-haired, overweight? You haven't seen her, have you?"

"Ha. You've got lots to learn about the way things work. You're still too close to life—you think the way people think. What's a wife? Sludge—in a shape of sorts, soft, squishy, with a pocket to reach into and pull babies out of, eh? What say we whip out to Mars and back? Want to race?"

"Another time maybe. I think I'll hang around some. Maybe I'll come across her."

"Fat chance."

"Well, see you later."

"There isn't any. You're a case. There should be a school for infants like you. Later, before, after, once upon a time: you'll stop thinking like that. Take a swoop or two out in the universe. Come back smarter, kid."

Guido eased through the glass, through the side wall of the church, and shot up over the city. He did a parabola, falling to, through, the roof of Santissima Annunziata. Ah, there below the altar, in a glass coffin, was the nun that Giacco had mentioned. Now for some answers. "Psst," he said. "Psst, Ambrosia!" She lay, or her body did, in classic repose, hands folded on her breast. Where her spirit was, who could say? Maybe she'd gone for a spin. Maybe she was lost in theological speculation. He couldn't get a word out of her.

He noticed a very old but familiar-looking woman kneeling at the altar before the coffin. "Mamma?" he said. He hovered before the wrinkled face. Then he saw the rings—her own, Laura's, and one on her right thumb, his. Could it be? This ancient creature was his daughter Lisa, whom he'd left just that morning in Via del Moro.

Her husband had died? Her daughter, too? For her to be wearing the rings, the whole family must have died. Had there been an epidemic? Were all the Iannottis dead?

He fired from the church and zipped straight to Via del Moro. In the apartment he found a strange young woman nursing a baby. Lisa must have moved. He didn't recognize any of the furniture. Thoughtfully, he cruised Via delle Belle Donne, Via della Spada, and the other streets in the maze off Piazza Santa Maria Novella. Paolo was gone, his shop converted to a shoestore, and though Fulvia's bakery was still there, he knew neither the owner nor the customers. On the facade of the church, pigeons still perched, but who knew how many generations of pigeons had lived and died since he'd lived in the quarter?

Had lived? Did live! He was more alive now than ever! Like a hummingbird, he shot straight up into the haze above the city. That meandering path of blue light down there—it was his beloved river, the Arno—and the big patch of green: what else but Cascine Park, where he and Laura had walked on Sunday when they were young. The red tile roofs, the broad boulevards, the parks, the labyrinthine narrow streets: that was Florence down there, filling the valley, busy as an anthill, lovely. With a city that complex and fascinating, why would he want a universe!

He tipped forward and shot down into it. This was where she would be—she'd loved the city as much as he did. Yellow was her color. Laura and yellow. Why else had he worn a yellow flower in his buttonhole for all those years? There, just above that border of jonquils—Laura?

No, but this was where she would come to—this park. The universe might be endless, but so was eternity. That improved the odds considerably. He wove among the yellow flowers, wove a pattern in the air above the grass, constructing an attractive design. The jonquils moved in the April breeze. He hovered brightly, giving off all the light he had.

Relative Motion

It was late morning, sunny, in April. Roger Cesare Innocenti was passing a cobbler's shop in Via della Spada. Straight across the street from him, not more than ten feet away, a man fell and lay on his back, eyes closed, his mouth working like the mouth of a beached fish. His face was the color of marble under dark clouds —dead gray—and his false teeth had slipped a little away from the gums. The right hand, callused and grimy, lay palm up, and the left lay palm down on the rough stones of the street. His suit, dark gray, had been worn until it looked like iron. His hat was still on his head, but tilted to the left. There was a yellow blossom in his buttonhole. Seventy-five or better, and done for. The gulping mouth brought no air into the lungs.

People didn't come running, they were already there, and they formed a knot around the fallen man. Their faces were fixed as in a painting, eyes wide, mouths slightly open, skin grayish. Shock: this was the real thing. A greengrocer held a large onion in his hand; the woman from the bakery across the street, wearing an apron over her dress, held both hands to her cheeks. In the second

circle were some tourists, and a bit farther back stood an American girl, or woman. She carried a plastic sack with OTTINO
printed on it and a Rome *Daily American.* She was wearing a
green sweater. The plastic sack, Roger would have bet, contained
a new leather handbag.

Someone had called the Misericordia. An ambulance turned in
from Piazza Santa Maria Novella, its siren deafening in the narrow street. It nosed through the crowd, then picked up speed and
departed. It was one of those ironies that Roger loved: wrong
ambulance, or wrong street, or wrong victim. This victim's jaw
was still twitching.

Another ambulance came then, without a siren—as if the first
one's siren had swept the way clear—and while the driver opened
the rear doors, a second man leaped out. When the two men
picked the corpse up, the hat fell off. The bald head was as white
as a sun-bleached skull. They slid, no, dumped him into the ambulance. The driver sailed the hat in after him. As the ambulance
moved off, the woman from the bakeshop said, *"È morto?"* Her
hands had left flour prints on her cheeks. The greengrocer, still
holding the onion, said *"Morto, sì."* The crowd dispersed.

Roger stayed. Smells: ripe pears, fresh baked bread, and something not so pretty, piss. There it was: a puddle where the corpse
had lain. Textures, yes—the rough stones of the buildings, iron
bars on the street-level windows, green shutters up above. The
yellowish April light touched everything, bringing out the surfaces. What, then, had happened? A branch had fallen into a
river, causing a momentary eddy, but then had floated away and
the stream continued.

He, too, continued. He was on his way to American Express to
cash some traveler's checks, but first he stopped at the Caffè Gilli,
on Piazza della Repubblica, for tea. In the leather notebook he
always carried, he wrote his impressions while they were still
fresh. Had the American girl been light- or dark-eyed? She'd had
dark hair and had stood with her weight mostly on one leg.

Which leg? She'd worn a raincoat, but had she carried an umbrella?

At any rate, a man had died, and the incident had brought a number of lives temporarily together, and then they had separated. While he sipped tea at Gilli, the American girl was in a different framework, she was somewhere else—and this fascinated him. If, say, she were on Lungarno Corsini about now, she might stop at a display window beside another dark-haired American girl, this one carrying a briefcase. The two women might look in at the same gray suede skirt and jacket, and then depart in opposite directions. This second woman would be Barbara, Roger's wife, and the first woman, without knowing it, would have encountered both husband and wife on the same morning.

* * *

In the mornings, Barbara went to the Dante Alighieri School for Foreigners, across the Arno, to study Italian. Roger spent the mornings out and around the city, keeping his eyes open, getting into conversations, taking notes. At one o'clock, they had lunch together, either in the apartment or at one of the nearby trattorias, and then they took a nap. At four o'clock they began their afternoon's work, Barbara preparing for the next day's class, Roger writing his daily article for the San Francisco *Courier*. He was committed to providing five pieces per week, but he did six, occasionally seven, to have something in reserve should hard times fall. He allowed himself four hours to turn out his fifteen hundred words. At 8 P.M. he and Barbara went out for dinner.

It was a plum of an assignment. He'd gotten it because he knew Italian, because he'd grown up in North Beach, and because his father, a second-generation Italian who owned an important restaurant on Columbus Avenue, was a longtime friend of Roger's editor. Even without connections, he probably would have landed the assignment. A sharp-eyed, dependable reporter in his midthirties, he had a bright future and his editor wanted that future to be with the *Courier*. He gave Roger virtual carte blanche in selecting material, just so it had an Italian flavor. He wanted to increase the *Courier*'s circulation in the Italian-American community.

The Innocentis had begun with a week in Palermo, and not an auspicious week. He knew Italian but not Sicilian. He couldn't get close to anyone, and though he recorded details of local color, he had no angle, no handle, no story. But then there was a murder in Agrigento, on Sicily's southern coast, so they rented a car and drove down. The victim was a public prosecutor who had been pressing the Mafia too hard, and this was retribution. He'd been shot in the back of the neck, at close range, while vacationing with his family. Roger and Barbara moved into the same hotel. Roger got interviews with the widow and the local carabinieri, all of whom did speak Italian, though they wouldn't say a lot. Barbara, who had taken a course in Organized Crime in Italy, contributed so much background that he was able to stretch the incident into a week's work—substantial stuff.

In Reggio di Calabria, across the Straits of Messina from Sicily, he did a piece on the legend that Odysseus had passed by there on his wanderings, that the straits were probably the famed Scylla and Charybdis, between which the wanderer nearly lost his life. At Barbara's suggestion, he wrote about the Riace Bronzes, two fifth-century B.C. Greek statues recently retrieved from the sea and now standing in Reggio's National Museum. The Greek influence was everywhere in the South of Italy, and he knew that Greek art informed both Roman and Renaissance art. He looked ahead to developing that theme, as they moved northward, in occasional thought pieces. It would get him into the museums and bring depth to his experience.

But he kept the *Courier*'s readership in mind, balancing heavy stuff with lighter stuff. There Barbara helped enormously. Her knowledge of gardening and cooking, her sensitivity to the place of women in society, broadened his scope, gave him an extra pair of eyes. At Cosenza she wrote her first solo story—on lace making —and at Bari, where Saint Nicholas is buried, she did one on the origin and history of Santa Claus.

They became a team, interspersing his work with hers. Roger's editor liked the idea, probably in part because he only paid Barbara a stringer's rate for her pieces. But her knowledge appeared in Roger's work as well. For years she'd been taking courses at one college or another, and it was astonishing how much she knew about a wide variety of things. What she didn't know, she could find. In their two weeks in Naples, they did three weeks' work, and the month in Rome gave them so much material that, if they'd wanted, they could have taken a month off to play.

Even in January, Sicily had been warm. Naples' weather had been about like San Francisco's. Rome in February was windy, and though there was sunshine, the air had a bite to it. Their week in Perugia, where they headquartered while exploring the Umbrian hills, was uncomfortably cold, and they arrived in Florence well ahead of spring. But in Florence they didn't have to stay in a hotel, at least; they used an apartment belonging to a friend of Roger's father, a tour director, who was off in Paris with a group of Americans. Here, at least, they could control the thermostat. They could spread out into several rooms and live like human beings for a change. Barbara enrolled in the Dante Alighieri School for the one-month short course. It wasn't just Italian she wanted, but Tuscan, the best Italian. She had studied French and Spanish, she knew Latin, and she hoped to end the month with Italian well in hand.

Roger had plenty to keep him busy. He did a piece on Lorenzo de' Medici, another on prostitutes, and one on "instant antique" shops. He wrote about the museums of Florence, about Michelangelo, about trattorias, the Central Market, transvestites, Italian films, piazzas, Sandro Botticelli, Florence's homeless, the train station, video arcades, the leather-goods industry. He had a fine eye for incongruities, and he knew how to buttress what he saw with what he read. So rich was the material here, he could never have captured it. In each day's newspaper were comedies and tragedies for a month of stories.

He and Barbara did see a tragedy. A theater company in Pistoia, only forty-five minutes away, was doing Sophocles' *Oedipus Rex.* Barbara thought it worth taking a break for, so they rode the train over for a Friday evening performance. They checked into a hotel, had dinner, then went to the theater. The theater was one of those nineteenth-century delights, oval in shape, with four rings of boxes above the main floor. The fronts of the boxes were painted ivory and trimmed in gold, and from the ceiling hung a magnificent chandelier. Barbara began taking notes as soon as they sat down, and she kept jotting, in the dark, during the performance. For once, Roger took no notes. He sat back and enjoyed the play, the rhythms, the nuances, so different in Italian than in the English productions he'd seen.

Afterward, he said, "How did you like it?"

"It was fine," she said. "The language was exquisite. That man really did marry his mother—I believe it. It seems to me that reality has to do with language. A thing isn't real until it's put into words."

"Be serious," he said. "Yesterday I saw a truck back up into one of those little Fiats. That was real."

"Then where is it now?"

He pointed to his temple.

"Is the truck in there?" she said. "The Fiat? The noise they made? No, to make it real, you would have to write it."

"Oh, come on," he said. "Most of the world's population don't write—they don't even read. Their lives are perfectly real."

"Are they? I don't know, Roger. When I look at my own life, even just yesterday or a week ago, it's pretty indistinct. My childhood is almost totally erased, except for a few incidents. I wouldn't say it was all that real."

"Don't you ever rest?" he said.

"Is something wrong?"

"Why should anything be wrong? Hell no, I'm fine. After Florence—Venice and Milan, and we're finished. Let's take a vacation somewhere, what do you say? Let's do absolutely nothing for a couple of weeks."

After breakfast the next morning, with two hours to kill before their train, they walked around Pistoia. It was a town as old as Florence, it had once been Florence's rival, but now, by comparison, it seemed a quiet little backwater. In the central piazza, they found the Saturday market in progress, the wide space crammed with small booths, with crowds shopping for the week. There seemed to be something going on over by the bell tower. Roger craned for a look. Barbara said, "Christ, a jumper."

Sure enough, there he was, high on the campanile, leaning over the railing, rocking back and forth, ready to let go at any second. He was wearing an orange vest, like a hunter or a railroad worker. The police were moving the crowd back. An ambulance arrived, and a party of men entered the tower at the bottom and began the long climb up to where the tiny figure stood. "Will he do it?" Barbara said.

"Let's go," he said. He took her arm.

"Are you crazy? Hey, I'm staying." She jerked free and said, "I'll meet you back at the hotel."

In a sort of daze, a suspension, he walked along the streets, noticing faces, colors, smells, sounds. Behind him, in another suspension, the man might be jumping, or might not. An hour later, when Barbara returned, Roger was lying on the bed, looking at the ceiling. "Are you okay?" she said. He was. He picked up their overnight bag, and they went down to the lobby to check out.

On the way to the train, she seemed different, taller, more forceful. Then he noticed. "New boots?" he said.

"Do you like them? I saw them in a window. Great price."

"What happened to the jumper?"

"Nothing. They got him down. No red splash or anything."

They went on to the station, Barbara striding a step ahead in her new high-heeled boots. Or could it have been that he was hanging back?

* * *

For four days, he'd been stuck on the story about the old man dying in the street. Everytime he revised the first paragraph, to sharpen the details, intensify the drama, he lost ground. The very facts seemed to evaporate beneath his fingers. He went back to where it had happened. From the woman at the bakery, he learned the dead man's name, Guido Iannotti, and that he'd been called The Old Man of the Quarter. A widower, he'd lived in Via del Moro, close by, and had walked in an old man's characteristic way, with his hands clasped behind his back.

But the greengrocer around the corner said that the old fellow had been called Yellow Flower, from his habit of wearing a blossom in his lapel. "He squeezed the pears," the greengrocer said. "He bruised ten to buy one. Now the pears are safe."

The more Roger learned, it seemed, the less he knew. Either the event was perfectly ordinary—a man had died after a long life—or it was something he didn't understand at all. For the first time in his career, he wasn't able to dive in and, with a surge of energy, finish a story. Did the old man's death mean something? All men die—Roger himself would keel over one day, in some far-off future. If that meant something, what did it mean? Or did it mean nothing?

He said, "Barbara, I'm bogged down. I can't seem to get this one rolling."

She looked up from her Italian lesson. "Oh? What is it?"

He showed her his notes. She said, "Hey, this is great. Do you mind if I have a try?"

She wrote it in two hours, by hand, then typed it up. He read it with astonishment. Though she'd used all of his details, even the American girl in the green sweater, what she'd written wasn't what he'd seen, but a version of it. It would sound true to anyone who hadn't been there, but not to the baker, the greengrocer, or the American girl. It would read absolutely true in the editor's office, so Roger signed it and mailed it off, but he was troubled. If one version was as good as another so long as the language made it seem true, then apples were oranges.

"You think too much," Barbara said. "No wonder you hit a wall."

Once again he saw the scene on the Lungarno, the American girl stopping by the shop window, Barbara stopping too, her briefcase in her right hand. But this time, Roger was with her between the two women, also looking in at the gray suede suit. He disengaged his right arm from Barbara's left, took the other girl's right arm with his left, and again the two women separated without speaking and walked off in opposite directions. Roger entered with a woman on his right arm, exited with a woman on his left, and each of the three would have a version of what had happened. All three versions would be valid, all true. In his, he would say, "My name is Roger Cesare Innocenti. I'll bet you have a new leather handbag in that sack." So his new life would begin.

* * *

It was a disease with a long gestation period. Suddenly it erupted. He ran a fever and had trouble breathing. An American was stabbed to death at Caffè Gilli, and his assailant shot by the police, and Roger couldn't get out of bed to cover the story. Barbara filled in for him, though it meant that she had to pop up at 4 A.M. to study Italian for her morning's class. She also covered a postal workers' strike and, somehow or other, managed to get her stories sent from the American Consulate, by diplomatic pouch, when no regular mail was moving. "My God," he said. "How did you do that?"

"I promised them an article—you know, the great service they give, the best of America abroad, that kind of thing. Background on American diplomacy, the commitment to NATO, et cetera. Notes from that old course I took."

"Well, thanks," he said. "I'll get on my feet pretty soon here."

She did the article on the consulate without leaving the apartment. The first draft was the final draft. It was good work, absolutely convincing. She shrugged off his compliments. "I had those journalism courses, you know."

When the Red Brigade, in a desperate rear-guard action, murdered two informers in Turin, she urged him to stay in bed, to let her handle it. She could do it blindfolded. She'd once written a paper on "Terrorism, Bakunin's Legacy in the Twentieth Century." It would be a matter of adding some particulars.

She was gone for four days. She returned with seven stories, one of them describing life inside a Red Brigade safe house. "Why, this is wonderful," he said. "You're a natural. How did you get these interviews?"

"A woman has certain advantages," she said. "She gives a little, receives a lot. Are you feeling better?"

"I think so. I think I'm about ready to get up, walk around some, start eating again."

"This telegram came," she said.

It was from Roger's editor, ecstatic over the new depth, new élan in the articles. Better yet, his work was receiving notice beyond San Francisco. Newspapers in Seattle, Chicago, and Boston were running his stories. Money was coming in. The editor was acting in his behalf. "Great news," Roger said. "I owe it all to you. Thanks, Barbara."

She said, "What about Milan and Venice—want me to do them?"

"Well, sure, if you want to. I'm really pretty weak still."

"I'd like to try, if you don't mind. You know something? After futzing around all these years, I think I've found my stride. I like this, I really do. But there's one thing. Roger . . ."

"Name it," he said. "You've saved my life. Ask and it's yours."

"It's a small thing, a matter of respect more than anything else. The byline?"

His surprise was momentary, and then relief flooded in. "You bet," he said. "I'll send a wire and explain."

"Well then, I'm off," she said. She looked at him tenderly. "I love you, Roger. You're a rare man."

"I'm not sure what I am, but I love you, too. When will you be back?"

"Let's leave it flexible. It depends on what happens. I'd say by the end of the month, at the outside."

"Okay. John and Martina are due back on May 1. I'll move to a hotel. I'll either be here or at the Baglioni, near the train station."

"May 1," she said wistfully. "How I'd love to be in Red Square."

He laughed and said, "Maybe next year."

"Maybe," she said. "Anything can happen. I'll tell you what let's do, though—that vacation you mentioned? Let's take a train through Yugoslavia. Dubrovnik—isn't that a great name? Let's stop off and nose around in Macedonia, work our way to Athens. Greece! What a history! Those bronze statues we saw in Calabria, they set me thinking. I really know quite a lot about Greece, but I'd like to see it with my own eyes. We could spend the summer. I'd like to take in the drama festival. I want to see *Oedipus* in Greek."

"We can't be gone that long. I'd be fired. I mean, you would."

"Let's quit. Listen, Roger, let's free-lance, see where it leads to. I've got all the confidence in the world. What do you say?"

"We'll talk about it when you come back."

"Good. But, Roger, I might decide to free-lance anyway, all right?"

They left it at that. She leaned over and kissed him, gave him a hug, and then departed. Was this the way things happened? These sudden alterations, changes of direction?

He was feeling better. He got out of bed, went to the bathroom, and showered away the sour sweat of his sickness. He shaved off his whiskers. He got dressed, picked up his umbrella, and went outside into a light rain.

The streets were choked with people moving to different purposes, frowning or smiling, impassive or enraged. Their faces only hinted at their secrets. Some of them talked to each other, some jabbered to no one at all, and some held their lips sealed tight. A woman made a furious, fisted gesture at the sky.

He walked and walked. The rain increased. Cars sent curtains of spray over the sidewalks. He found himself smiling, chuckling, laughing. Where was Barbara by now? Wherever she was, there, too, was the load. He himself carried nothing. It was as if he'd met her at the center of a bridge, transferred the weight to her hand from his, and continued freely while she carried the burden back the way he'd come, into his past.

Though it was dark in the streets now, there were still lots of people out, and he didn't understand one of them. Their umbrellas crawled here and there like black bugs. If he wasn't mistaken, he saw a priest crossing a piazza, disrobing as he went. But he might have been mistaken. He laughed aloud. It was a peculiar sound, a kind of croaking. Something squished underfoot. He'd stepped in big dogshit. His best shoes, too. But there was water in the gutter. He thrust his foot in to the ankle, swished his shoe around, then stamped on the curb. He laughed. He went laughing through the incomprehensible streets.

Men Are Like Children,
Like the Beasts

It was a Florence dream, a distortion of something she'd actually seen on the street: a dump truck, with two men standing by, pouring coal down a chute into a basement. But as she dreamed it, one man pressed close behind her, reached under her arms and took her breasts in his hands, and then, with his knee between her legs, lifted her onto the chute. Down she went, clawing the coal, to where there was no light at all.

She woke up fighting the covers. The rattling she heard was the windows shaking as a truck rolled by on Via della Vigna Nuova, three stories below. She heard another sound then—a cup on a saucer. It was 5 A.M., but her father was up. He got by on naps, day and night, and was up day and night, reading, writing. The nurse, Signora Tinelli, urged him to take the prescribed sleeping pills, to rest and save his strength. But he said, "I'll catch up on sleep later."

Laura got up and put her robe on. In the kitchen, she found him, in baggy pants and an old gray sweater, making tea. "Did I wake you?" he said. "Sorry."

"It was a truck going past," she said. "With all the stone in these buildings, you wouldn't think anything could shake them."

"No flexibility—solid," he said. "This one has been here for five centuries. Coffee?"

"I'll make it. You sit down. Sit—I mean it!"

He sat. "Bossy, aren't you? Like your mother."

"Don't say that, Alex. I'm not like her at all."

"In that blue robe, you look like her. It's her favorite color, or used to be. You resemble her in lots of ways. You stand like her, with your head cocked to one side, frowning."

She poured the espresso into a large cup, sweetened it, then filled it with hot milk. In the bluish fluorescent light, he looked awful. His face was dead gray, with a blue-black band of broken capillaries across his nose and cheeks. He'd lost hair from the treatments, and the little he had left, in a fringe around his ears and a few strands on top, was silver and spiritless. His sunken cheeks made the mouth protrude. It was as if he were wearing a mask. She said, "Let's go to the living room, okay?"

There, in the lamplight, he seemed ruddier, but his hand trembled as he set the cup and saucer on the coffee table. "I meant it as a compliment, Laurie. Esther was pretty at your age. You're pretty."

"Well, she's not pretty now. She's rich. She got what she wanted—Jake and his money."

"She's persistent," he said. "That's not a bad quality to have. You're persistent."

"Look, Alex, you're lucky she divorced you. It was the best thing that ever happened. It changed your life."

"That it did," he said, "—and yours. How many American kids spend part of every year in Florence? It was good for you, wasn't it? Didn't it give you more dimensions? In your stories, you know,

(23)

there's an ease, a sophistication. I think it's because you did all that traveling when you were a kid."

"Maybe," she said.

"No, I mean it. I think it was for the best, for all of us, in all respects. Esther's happy, I changed my life—I haven't had a drink now for fifteen years. And you, well, you're not the child of an ordinary American home. You've had some experience. You've got things to write about. Take this, for example—it's another experience, grist for the mill."

"This isn't grist for anything, Alex. Do you remember an old tweed coat you used to have, out at the elbows? After you left, I took it to bed with me every night, and I was twelve years old, for Christ's sake. Esther caught me at it, and the next day I found myself at a lady psychiatrist's. Now you're leaving again. I know —it's no one's fault. It wasn't then, it isn't now—it's just life. But it's not just to write stories about."

"Maybe not, for ordinary people. But you're not ordinary, sweetie. You've got a gift, if you'll only use it. Those stories of yours, they're well done, the surfaces are brilliant, like varnish. If they were someone else's, I'd say, 'Not bad—here's a talent.' But I know you, I know you're not reaching down underneath, you're not taking chances. You're making them up. Never once, in the whole book, does your own pain come into it."

"So you're a critic."

"Of a sort, yes. I read a lot, books are my business. But I'm your father, and I don't find any detail in those ten stories like that of the girl who takes her father's jacket to bed. Now what I'm saying is, go all the way—commit yourself. Open up and tell the truth. There are hundreds of books like yours, amusing, well written, witty language. But there aren't many like the one you could write, if you'd let yourself. So you won a prize. You didn't come anywhere near your limits. You've got to push yourself, test yourself, find the end of what you can do."

"There are other things in life, Alex. Michael, for one. I think a whole lot of Michael. If we're going to have a family, we'd better get started. I'm twenty-seven, I should have the first one before I'm thirty."

He smiled and it was like a death's-head. His teeth gleamed in the light. He sank back in the chair. His voice came out from there. "If I were you, I would write the story of a young woman who, because her father was a boozer, because he ran out on her when she was twelve, tries desperately to hold her own marriage together. Her husband is a little like her father, but not a boozer. He's a professor, as her father used to be, but a good one, a real scholar, and she wants his children."

"Alex, Dad—"

"That's what I would do, if I were you and had your gift."

He didn't say any more. He sat there, limp. "Are you tired?" she said.

"I'm always tired. That's the trouble with this goddamn dying. Shit, I guess I'd better have a nap—and I just got up."

He leaned forward, and she jumped to help him. His arm inside the thick sweater felt like strings on a stick. When he was on his feet, he shook free and said, "I can make it." He tried stepping out, but his leather slippers shuffled on the carpet. He could barely hold his head up. He got into the hallway, though, and she heard his bedroom door click shut. "Goddammit," she said, for the bad times were just beginning.

* * *

Alexander Angel, Alessandro Delangelo, had changed his name, along with everything else, when at age thirty-nine he left America for good. He chose Florence because his grandfather had come from there, immigrating to an Italian neighborhood in the Bronx. His father, when his turn came, had escaped to New Haven, changed his name to Angel, and opened an automotive garage. Alex was the youngest of three sons, and his father had given them all a good education; he didn't want them to spend their lives digging grease from their fingernails. They should be professional men. Of the older two, one was a lawyer, the other an accountant with his own firm. Alex, with a literary imagination and a taste for philosophy, earned a Ph.D. at Yale, then took a job at the State University of New York at Binghamton.

But something went wrong with Alex. He himself didn't know what it was, and it crept up on him so slowly that he couldn't be sure it was anything at all until, all of a sudden, it was everything. He couldn't remember being totally sober, really dried out. His career, after a brilliant beginning, had vanished into a desperate hanging on from day to day, while he tried to make his lectures. He hadn't written anything for five years. How could it have happened? He was such a witty, friendly, intelligent man. But somehow he'd become one of those permanent associate professors who never do anything scandalous enough to be fired but who, like a leak in the hold of a ship, keep everyone pumping to save their lives.

He hadn't intended it to be that way. He hadn't intended to hurt his wife or anyone else, himself least of all. No, his daughter least of all. He would have done anything to keep from hurting her. He would have thrown himself into fire, would have endured any torture, would have sacrificed himself gladly. But he hurt her nevertheless, hurt his wife and himself, hurt everyone who had anything to do with him. His wife left him, took his daughter back to New Haven, and moved in with her parents, humiliated. It was summer when that happened; he had no classes to meet, so he stayed drunk for two weeks, a month, and woke up on a street in Boston, dead sick, sick to the roots of his soul. He had apparently been trying to find New Haven.

It was his body that sent him to the hospital. He was vomiting blood, shitting blood, and he panicked at the thought that he might die in the street. His heart bumped and twittered, and he had the shakes to the point where he could barely walk, but he made it to the hospital. He convinced them that he had insurance;

he begged for help, literally begged. He was employed, he said, and gave them the name of the university. They checked with his department chairman and admitted him.

It was while in the hospital, off booze, that the truth came to him. It was something anyone could have told him, but it came like absolute lightning, like God speaking in a dream: "Take your choice, live or die." It was as clear as a fork in the road. He could go one way or the other—it was up to him.

Knowledge was one thing, action another thing entirely. Between the two came the will. To protect him from himself, he checked into a clinic for a month's grace while he built up strength. He summed up his assets; they came to very little. Esther would get the house, car, the shabby furniture; she could have his library. That was about it. He had thrown, spent, pissed it all away. Could he ever be strong enough to stay straight? No, not here, not in America, and not anywhere else, either, unless he got help from some power beyond himself.

He wasn't religious. He had left the church when he was fourteen, he didn't believe in God, and he loathed those alcoholics, like many at the clinic, who suddenly found faith and proclaimed it loud and long. He didn't loathe them as he would've loathed himself for doing it, but they put him on edge. They undercut his resolve by making fools of themselves. Still, he had to grant them the right to be fools, to scream hallelujah all day long, to do anything, anything to stay sober, to hang on one more day without a drink.

The father he confessed to was his own. He laid it all out, spared the man nothing, flayed himself, and asked to borrow ten thousand dollars. "For what? Booze?" his father said. "No, I want to go to Italy and start all over. Not a drop, I swear." His father gave him a long look, steady, neither believing nor disbelieving, then said, "Okay." That was all he said. He wrote out the check.

What a father! What a man! The son, though, was a boozer with ten grand in his pocket. From New Haven to Binghamton, the road was lined with bars, party stores, restaurants, motels. He kept his foot on the accelerator, his eyes straight ahead. It was even dangerous to stop for a traffic light. In Binghamton he drove straight to the university and resigned, ceding his retirement fund to his wife. He went to a lawyer and had divorce papers drawn: everything to Esther Angel, including one of the two paychecks he still had coming. The other he would use for one-way plane fare to Rome.

He called Esther, then, and told her what he'd done. She could come back to the house, it was safe, he would be gone. She said, "You sonofabitch, Alex. You no good, worthless bastard." He asked if he could see Laura before he left. Her refusal was like a steel door. He didn't press. He didn't have a leg to stand on.

He stayed only until he got his passport and had signed what needed signing. He paid off his lawyer, and with something over nine thousand dollars in his pocket, he took a bus to New York City. He had a suitcase and a briefcase. The books in his office, his books and papers at home, the rest of his clothes in drawers and closets—let Esther deal with those as a widow would. He left his death behind him and, like an immigrant, went to Florence. Like his grandfather, he didn't have the language of his adopted country, which made him a virtual innocent in a very complicated, even Byzantine bureaucracy.

His grandfather had known fruit, his father knew cars, and Alex knew books, but not from the business angle. Still, what else was there? He found a lawyer who spoke English and proposed a partnership in a small book store, specializing in English editions. The lawyer thought it might be worth a try. He matched Alex's investment and undertook the tortuous procedures for starting a business in Florence.

The lawyer, Enzo Bonsignori, received no return on his investment for quite a while. As for Alex, he lived on virtually nothing in the storeroom of the small shop in Piazza Carlo Goldoni. It was the same thing his grandfather had done in New York while learning the language, learning to do business in a foreign city.

Enzo Bonsignori turned out to be an honest man, and Alex, by living on almost nothing, was able to expand his stock, pay a little on the debt to his father, and bring Laura over once a year for a visit, either for two weeks at Christmas or a month in the summer. Within five years he had an apartment, in seven he'd paid his father off, and in ten he'd bought his partner out. By then he was a naturalized Italian citizen, with the name Alessandro Delangelo, and owner of this very nice apartment on Via della Vigna Nuova, close to the store.

Laura knew part of this history, but only part; the rest she read in his study, at his insistence—fifteen thick journals, one for every year he'd lived in Florence. As she read his day-to-day thoughts, she had the peculiar sensation of being watched by a shadow, as if in a mirror she were seeing both herself and this translucent shape behind her—ghost or spirit—that moved as she moved, turned as she turned, and was still alive in the next room. It made her queasy. "I'm not sure I want to do this, Alex," she said. But he said, "Do it. What other kid gets a chance to ask her father questions, penetrate the parental mystery, and so on?"

"Some of this is private—intimate."

"You bet it is. Otherwise it wouldn't be true."

He had fallen in love twice, but couldn't bring himself to marry again because, in his mind, marriage was associated with disaster. On the other hand, prostitutes left him feeling desolated. He'd had gonorrhea three times, he'd suffered from hemorrhoids since age twenty-five, and seven years ago he'd had a mild heart attack. Every day of the fifteen years he'd craved alcohol. On his bulletin board she found a quotation from Heraclitus: "Whenever a man gets drunk, he is led by a beardless boy, stumbling, not knowing whither he goes, for his soul is wet. It is a delight to souls to become wet."

When she'd finished, he said, "Any questions?"

"No. You were lonely. You loved me. You had some very bad times."

"True, true, and true," he said.

That had been two weeks ago, when he was feeling better. Now they had talked themselves out. They'd covered everything, held nothing back. They were as close as they would ever be, perhaps as father and daughter could be. There was nothing to do now but wait.

* * *

When Signora Tinelli arrived at eight o'clock, Alex was still resting. Busty, middle-aged, and taciturn, the signora seemed capable of handling any number of difficult matters at the same time. Alex's doctor had recommended her, and Laura liked her; she was practical, efficient, and motherly—in a no-nonsense way. She came now during the days, but later would move into the third bedroom to be there nights as well.

Over coffee, Laura brought her up to date, and then she wrote a long letter to Michael, more for her own good than to tell him of new developments. There were no new developments. The progress of leukemia is inevitable and foreseeable—a steady deterioration, increasing pain—and the shock of what was coming, while she stood by helplessly, she had already imagined as clearly as if she'd seen a film of it. So she wrote for stability, to keep herself level, placed in time. The month she'd been here seemed like a year, and Michael seemed so far in the past that she could barely remember what he looked like.

When at ten o'clock Alex still hadn't appeared, she got into her raincoat, told the signora she would be right back, and started for the post office. She took the elevator down and stepped into the street. The weather hit her. Spring had moved in overnight. The sun was warm, the air moist and balmy, the sky a strip of brilliant blue above the tall houses.

It sucked the strength right out of her. Instead of turning left toward the post office, she strolled to Piazza Carlo Goldoni and stood looking into the window of Alex's bookstore. There were customers, the clerks moved around busily, and it didn't seem possible that he hadn't just stepped out for a moment, perhaps for an espresso at the Bar Goldoni. Or maybe he was in the store-room, opening cartons from London and New York. The books in the window had been dusted. Florence was a dirty city. He fought a constant battle against dust.

She walked to the Arno at the foot of the Carraia Bridge, then turned left and went beside the slow brown river. The houses on the other side—just yesterday drab walls with windows—the sun teased into fine distinctions of color, shades of beige, mustard, yellow-orange, and ocher. Green shutters stood open, windows stood open, and curtains fluttered in the mild breeze.

In the shop windows, everything looked lovely—the linens, draperies, leather goods, antique furniture, men's clothes, wom-en's bright spring cottons. In one window was an outfit of dove gray suede—hat, jacket, skirt, and shoes—and as she looked at it, she caught the reflection of her green sweater in the glass. It reminded her of Michael's green canvas book bag. Two years ago he'd lost his briefcase in the subway; he'd set it down on the platform and it disappeared. "Not smart," he said, and went back to using the green sack.

The sun on her shoulders, a breeze in her hair, she followed the Arno to the Ponte Vecchio, and then turned left toward the post office. After she mailed her letter, she began looking.

Within four blocks of the post office, there were probably thirty leather-goods stores, with hundreds of briefcases. But this one, for Michael, would have to speak to her. She went into shop after shop and saw many beautiful things, but not the right thing. Again and again she said, "Yes, but no." As she came out of Via de' Rondinelli, though, she saw it in the window of the shop across the street. OTTINO was the name above the window, and what she wanted stood on the middle shelf. When the light changed, she went directly into the store. She brought a clerk outside and pointed.

With hundreds of cases on his shelves, the clerk was amused to have to take off his shoes and go into the window for this one. He was a young man, pleased to be waiting on a young woman. He handed her the case and watched as she ran her fingers over the rich leather, smelled it, put her hand inside and felt the kidskin lining. "I'll take it," she said. "How much?"

He showed her the tag. It was a lot more than she had.

"Credit card?" she said.

He took the card and made out the slip. As she signed it, he said, "Laura Angel—an appropriate name."

"Thank you," she said.

He wrapped the briefcase in tissue paper, then put it into a plastic carrying bag. *"Grazie, signora. Buon giorno."*

"Buon giorno," she said.

Outside, she looked at her watch: nearly noon. What if Alex had gotten up right after she left? Then she would have wasted two hours she could have spent with him, wasted them in pleasing herself. She hadn't thought about him since ten o'clock, except in the store, when she saw how much the briefcase cost. First, she'd thought: Well, anything for Michael. Then that ugly second thought had flickered in: Alex will leave me some money. Laura Angel indeed, trading the dead for the living.

She hurried along now, taking the shortest way. She left the wide Via de' Tornabuoni and cut through by a narrow, sunless street whose high-walled houses trapped the odors of food and excrement. In here were no terraces, no gardens, but only a few green plants set desperately in window boxes. This was a section of medieval Florence. The streets met at odd angles, and urine reeked in the alleys. No one living in here could forget his basic humanity.

On Via della Spada, a hot breath came from a slit of a doorway —the smell of meat roasting—and then she saw a clump of people gathered around something on the ground. A man was down. He didn't seem to have fallen; he might have sat, then lain back on the sidewalk. His hat was still on his head. So old he seemed almost translucent, he was frail and decorous, his face composed, his worn suit buttoned formally, with a jonquil at the lapel.

The crowd wore a complex, collective expression of shock: a man was dying, had just then died, right before their eyes. It was a moment of horror and, at the same time, a thrill: someone else had died, not themselves. They couldn't see enough of it; they greedily stored up the sight. At the edge of the cluster stood a man whose expression was particularly intense. He might have been smelling food after a month's starvation. His eyes darted nakedly from the dead man to the people watching. They rested for an instant on Laura, as if she were a dessert he might get around to after he'd slaked on flesh.

The dead man's mouth had opened, the false teeth had slipped, and the jaw still moved a little, out and in. But even so, he looked seemly. He had come naturally to the end of a long life; he'd been allowed to keep some dignity. Lucky man. In the form on the pavement, there was no trace of the horror that lay ahead for Alex, the nightmare he would fight through to reach the end.

She shivered, then squeezed past the crowd. A little farther on, she had to retreat into a doorway to let an ambulance go by. No, two ambulances, the first with a siren, the second silent. The first one kept going and disappeared in the direction of the post office. It was for the living. The silent one stopped.

She took Via del Moro toward the river and came out not far from the apartment. At a florist's, she bought a dozen jonquils. Alex liked yellow. As she was leaving, she turned back on impulse, and bought another dozen. He deserved all the yellow she could bring him.

In the apartment, she found Signora Tinelli grating cheese in the kitchen. "He's not feeling well, he's asleep again."

"Did he eat?"

"A little soup, not much. And the medicine gives him constipation."

Laura put the flowers in vases.

"*Giunchiglie*—jonquils," the signora said. "How pretty."

* * *

It was four-thirty in the afternoon and still warm on the balcony, the terrazzo above the courtyard. On the top floor of the building, they still had the sun, but dusk had already come to floors below. Alex sat in a canvas deck chair, wrapped to his chin in a blanket, his eyes half closed. Signora Tinelli had placed the two vases of jonquils on a bench in front of him. As the sun sank, the light thickened and the flowers slowly deepened to gold.

Laura thought he was falling asleep again, but he spoke, "You know, there's a way out of this. A man I knew did it. He was my lawyer's brother, heavy smoker, lung cancer. While he still could, he invited his friends and family in for a big party, and said good-bye to each of them. Then he retired to his bedroom and took his medicine—his cure-all. He spared everyone's sensibilities, particularly his own. Except, of course, that as a Catholic he sent his soul to hell by doing it."

"Could you do it?" she said.

"It's attractive—and I could do it, you bet I could. I've turned it over in my mind again and again. But it's strange—where my friend believed in the soul, and did it anyway, I don't believe in the soul and won't do it. I just don't want to cheat—it comes down to that."

"Cheat?" she said. "That wouldn't be cheating. God almighty, Alex—"

"I mean cheating myself. Cutting myself off before my time. Missing something. If I were going to have a gravestone, which I'm not, I'd like my epitaph to read, 'Here lies a man who lived it to the last.' I mean all of it, all I've been allotted."

"Alex, you've lived it, haven't you? It seems to me—"

"Have I? I don't know. How do you measure the quality of a life?"

"Maybe there isn't such a thing as 'a life,' " she said. "Maybe there's only 'a life right now.' Right now the quality is high, isn't it? It is for me."

He thought for a moment, then laughed. "You're pretty smart, for a kid."

Then his lids drooped and he fell asleep. She waited. These sudden naps never lasted long. He would drop into unconsciousness, then snap back. Across the courtyard, the sun balanced on the tile roof, a red ball shimmering, pulsing, dangerous-looking. It turned the jonquils yellow-orange, and put red into the walls and on the backs of her hands. Alex's head and face looked as if he'd spent the day at the beach, burning.

"Everything's arranged," he said. "Enzo will take care of it. There's an insurance policy—you're the beneficiary. The store and this apartment—Enzo will sell them, half to go to him, half to you. Now what that means is you'll have enough to quit your job and live in Italy for a couple of years, maybe more, if you stretch it. Michael could take a leave of absence. Anyway, think of it as a grant, a writing fellowship, your chance to test yourself. The kicker is you can't take the money out of Italy—it's the law. You have to spend it here."

"Alex . . ."

"Quit that job. You're no social worker—you're a writer, or could be. If Michael won't come, leave him. Damn it, use yourself right, use yourself up. Don't get stuck making babies for Michael."

"He'll come, Alex. I don't have to leave him. I'm not stuck."

"Goddammit!" he said. A fleck of saliva gleamed at the corner of his mouth. His lips pushed out and back, as if he'd felt something on his tongue.

The light was leaving the jonquils—they were already dark yellow—and gray slid up the blanket, rising over his face. The light, reflected in the tall window behind them, shone briefly like a red cap on the skin of his head, then went out, and he was all gray.

He said, "I want you to leave tomorrow morning. Take the nine o'clock train to Rome. Your flight to New York leaves at 4 P.M.—it'll get you there in time for a late dinner."

"No you don't, Alex—I'm staying. I'm seeing this all the way through. There's no way you're going to get rid of me."

"Don't think I'm doing this to spare your feelings," he said. "It's purely selfish. With you here, I talk. We cover the same ground over and over. Now I want to stop talking. I don't want to talk again."

"Then we won't talk. I can shut up."

"I want to be by myself," he said. "I want to think, sink into myself, and see if I can find my soul. Please go—for my sake. We've had a wonderful visit—I wouldn't have missed it for the world. But this once, don't be stubborn. Be a dutiful daughter. Now, help me up. Let's go inside. It's cold as a witch's tit out here."

* * *

He had no appetite at dinner. He drank a cup of chicken broth, then went to bed. She thought over what he'd said, but couldn't make up her mind. Of course, she could have it both ways by moving to a pensione and keeping in touch through Signora Tinelli. It wouldn't be quite aboveboard, but then she would be there if he changed his mind. He might want her when things got really bad, might be glad to have her hold his hand.

She held off on packing her things. She went to bed and slept, for once, without dreaming. She got up at six and made coffee. She found his cup in the sink. He'd come and gone. He wasn't in the study.

At seven Signora Tinelli arrived. Laura said, "You're early—what's going on?"

"I don't know. He called last night and asked me to come. Wait, I'll find out."

She was gone for a good fifteen minutes. When she returned, her face was flushed. "That man—impossible," she said. "He gave me this, for you."

It was another notebook, with an envelope sticking out. In the envelope, she found a plane ticket and a note. The note said, "I hate good-byes. No scenes, now, okay? Pack up and head home. Sweets, I've loved you all your life."

"I want to see him," she said.

"He locked the door. He won't see you. I'm supposed to help you pack, then call a taxi."

She went to his door and tried it. It was locked. She called, "Alex!" He didn't answer. It was ridiculous. "All right—I'll go," she said. "Just let me in to say good-bye!"

There wasn't a sound from inside.

She went to her room and packed her things. Then she told the signora to call a cab. She went to the door again and hit it with her fists. "I'm going—I'm all packed. Let me in, Alex—let me give you a hug. Dad, I love you!"

No response. Nothing. Signora Tinelli gave her a handkerchief for her eyes, then pulled her firmly. "He knows, child," she said. "He hears every word."

There was no point in blubbering. There was nothing more she could do. She picked up her suitcase and said good-bye to the signora. She said, "Take care of him."

"That's my job. Don't worry, I will. *Auguri*—good luck."

Her eyes flooding, Laura carried her things to the elevator.

* * *

On the train to Rome, she watched hills and towns roll by. She barely moved for the whole four hours. She didn't look into the notebook, she sat stupefied, and from the Rome terminal she mechanically took the bus to the airport. As she boarded the jet, she said, "Well, it's over."

The jet lifted and she shot westward over the Mediterranean.

The notebook—hell, it was empty. She flipped through the blank pages. Then, on the last page, she found it. It was dated that day; he must have written it while having tea, early that morning.

> Thanks for seeing it my way, sweets. Second thoughts on the epitaph. Here's a dandy from Heraclitus. "Men are not awake; they resemble those who are in deep sleep, or they may be likened to the drunken; they are like children, or like the beasts." Enough said, eh? I love you, I'm behind you all the way. Look ahead. Have a drink for me!
>
> Alex

That letter she'd mailed to Michael: she would arrive before it did. It might even be on the plane with her. The briefcase was, for sure—she'd packed it between layers of clothing in her luggage. Evening it would be, April, the windows open to the sounds from the street. She allowed herself to hope for soft weather.

She caught the flight attendant's attention. She said, "Please bring me a double vodka, no ice—just spirit, pure spirit."

Uccello

This time he is arrested for shaking a street sign, for shouting, for cracking a tourist's ribs. The tourist forced him off the sidewalk, and Uccello took vengeance with an elbow. The air whooshed from the foreigner's lungs, he bent over, cried out, and Uccello became too excited. He leaped and grabbed the metal pole of a street sign, flung his weight back and forth, and harangued his fellow citizens: "Florentines, arise! Throw those bastards out!"

The arresting officer, new to the job, knows no better than to put handcuffs on Uccello and cart him to the station. In the back of the police car, he thrashes, a hawk in a cage. "Traitor, fool, imbecile!" he rages. "Foreign spy!" The officer, who is barely old enough to shave, drives grimly. In the courtyard of the *questura,* he takes his prisoner by the nape of the neck, shakes him like a feather duster, brings him before the sergeant.

The sergeant rolls his eyes. "You again, Uccello. What did you do this time?"

The young one says, "He attacked a tourist. He tried to destroy public property. He created a disturbance, used abusive language, resisted arrest."

"Is this true, Uccello?"

"Foreigners occupy the city, and you do nothing. You put patriots in chains."

"There are laws," says the sergeant. "I uphold the laws, which protect both strangers and Florentines." He observes Uccello sternly. "Do you remember the tight jacket, the locked doors, the injections?"

A clerk enters the office and drops a folder on the sergeant's desk. The sergeant says, "Here between these covers is your life, Uccello. Shall I take this file to the judge, or will you be good?"

"I'll be good."

"No more temper tantrums, eh?"

"No, on my honor, sir—no tantrums."

"Leave the tourists alone? No wild speeches? Do you remember the electricity?"

Uccello's neck tightens. "I promise, sir."

"Then go, before I change my mind. I don't want to see you here again." The sergeant stands up behind the desk, a huge man with gray hair and a gray mustache. He leans forward like an old wall.

Uccello turns, finds the door, and flies from the office. He crosses the courtyard. Holding his breath, he passes the two sentries at the gate. Miraculously, they don't shoot him, though they have carbines to shoot with if they wish.

On the street then, and safe, he controls his thoughts by walking with one foot on the curb, the other in the gutter. A shout rises in his throat, but he bites its head off. He bobs up and down, staring at the curb just ahead. He jams his fists into his pockets. A shout escapes from his lips and he bites off its tail.

Back in the office, Sergeant Garbari says to the young officer, "I see you disapprove. You think this Uccello should be locked up because the law is the law."

Officer Mulinaro does disapprove, and for that reason. But he hasn't advanced to where he is by challenging his superiors. He opens the file to the cover sheet, then says, "Uccello Uccello, who is he? What kind of name is that?"

"He's a casualty," says the sergeant. "He's nobody. He showed up in a hospital just after the war, memory gone, in shock. No one ever claimed him. He gave himself the name Uccello. He took the name twice, he told me, so that if he forgot one, he would still have the other. His existence, let's say, is provisional. He lives in the streets, like lots of other people. True, he hates foreigners, but is that a crime? I'm not too fond of them myself."

"You don't assault them, you don't rant."

The sergeant looks past the young man. "Uccello and I are of the same generation. In the last weeks of the war, the Germans were destroying the country as they retreated to the North. Italians fought against Italians, Fascists against partisans, killing one another in the fields, the streets. Insanity! Brutality! What a terrible time! All who survived bear the marks, believe me."

These old uncles, the young officer thinks—they're full of reminiscences. They don't live in the present. The arrest record of this Uccello, Bird, Simpleton, has violence on every page. He hasn't injured anyone yet, it's true, but his threats and wildness have put him behind bars on several occasions. He has been in and out of the mental facility. "I wouldn't call him harmless, Sergeant. He could do real damage."

The sergeant shrugs. "If we arrested people for the crimes they could commit, the entire population would be in jail, you and I among them." He looks directly at the young man. "You are intelligent. You are strong and you have courage. Try to learn compassion." He gestures, and the officer is dismissed.

To Officer Mulinaro's way of thinking, the old sergeant is blind to the city. Everywhere one looks, there are whores and pimps, thieves, pickpockets, and beggars. Filthy Gypsies squat shamelessly on the sidewalks, clutching at decent people's clothing. Vagrants sleep in the train station, in doorways, under the bushes in the piazzas. They live on garbage. Shouters, haranguers, and threateners infest the city—crazy people of both sexes. Decent people can't walk the streets without confronting this trash. Seven million tourists a year come to taste the famed beauty of Florence, and are besieged at every step by human trash.

Human trash, like any other trash, should be disposed of. How else to make Florence worthy of her name? It isn't time yet—the old uncles still hold the upper hand—but the day will come when law will prevail, when there won't be a speck of dirt in sight, when this beloved city will again be the world's envy.

* * *

Uccello's way lies through the city center. In the Piazza della Repubblica, he falls in behind a group speaking German, a language that sounds like feet stuck in mud, like a pump struggling in a cellar. It's hardly a language at all. At the head of the group, the leader, a heavy woman in a flowered dress, turns in at the Caffè Gilli. The sheep follow, and Uccello, unable to escape, finds himself under the canopy amid the wealthy.

English, French, and German he recognizes, but he hears other tongues that he wouldn't try to guess at. They are black, brown, or yellow, according to the color of their speakers. From the mouths of the Italian waiters, he hears obsequious speech. Money changes hands. Dishes are being served. The foreigners are buying Italy. At every table, Italy is being sold by these bowing, unctuous waiters in white jackets. The foreigners: what rich clothing, what fat wallets! How casually they order fancy drinks, salads, heaping desserts! They have wads of lire in every pocket!

The Germans follow their leader to a long table, leaving Uccello exposed in the aisle. He finds himself looking at a face in profile. It seems scarcely human. It slopes like a hillside, creased and eroded; it's swollen; it's as red as scraped earth. It looks like a rubber carnival mask. The man wearing it fills his chair like a fat sack of pork, and he stares at his drink with tiny, piggish eyes.

Has Uccello seen that face before? He stands still as a heron.

The man lifts a fat hand and waves a banknote, and one of the waiters scrambles over, shiny as a rat. The man laboriously rises from his chair, speaking English. English? Shouldn't he speak German? But he wouldn't dare, though he's German through and through. Uccello suddenly recognizes him beneath that ruined face.

"Betrayer!" The word escapes before he can lock his lips. The waiter growls, "Begone, shoo, vanish," and flaps his napkin as at a pigeon. Fat Hermann has moved off, is leaving the café. He walks peculiarly, lifting each foot as though stepping up on a curb. Uccello exults. He shouts at the swinish back, "Traitor!"

The man keeps going. Uccello follows him to the newsstand in the loggia and stops, close enough to touch his coat, while he buys a paper. Over Hermann's arm, he reads the headlines. Hermann grunts, "Unk!" and brings the news close to his face. His hands are shaking—the paper trembles. Uccello's eyes aren't what they once were. What has caught the traitor's attention? Hermann grunts again, then waddles off, the paper folded under his arm. Uccello follows, a crow trailing a corpse wagon.

At the end of Via de' Panzani, they turn right, then right once more, and Hermann enters the Grand Hotel Baglioni. Uccello knows better than to try getting past the doorman. He crosses to the center of the Piazza dell'Unità Italiana and perches on the steps of the monument. His view includes the whole front of the hotel.

* * *

Different laws govern the rich and the poor, the powerful and the weak, the fatfolk and leanfolk. Hermann can follow his whims, while Uccello must wait. All afternoon he sits watching the door, while the betrayer, his purse bulging with money wrung from Italy, stuffs his paunch in the hotel's restaurant and has a nap in a comfortable suite behind one of the arched windows, probably on the top floor. Uccello's buttocks are stringy—the bones push right through. He goes numb with waiting.

The hour passes when, in Via della Spada, he can usually count on handouts from the baker, the grocer, the cheese vendor. Darkness falls over his hunger. The dinner hour goes by. In April, however warm the days, the nights bring a chill from the mountains. Uccello wraps himself in his arms. Hermann might not emerge for a week, might swill in the hotel and wallow in his soft bed, calling for anything his fat desires.

But just when Uccello has firmed his mind for an all-night vigil, the door opens and the huge form oozes through—and into a taxi! Before Uccello can unbend, the taxi has gone! The rich can do anything; they can betray their friends with impunity, and after their friends are dead and the cause lost, they can return to gorge and guzzle. Years after their throats should have been cut, here they are in big hotels, snuffling and grunting, at the very scene of their crime.

Since Hermann took no luggage, he'll be back tonight. Uccello is free for a few hours, to eat and get warm. He straightens up and gets his hips going. To move his blood, he swings his arms out and flaps them up and down. He unlocks his throat as he walks, flies, along Via de' Panzani. Well in advance, he lets everyone know who's coming. "Uccello Uccello, Double Bird, Double Idiot!" Don't people step out of his way?

At a bar, he alights, and the man behind the counter says, "Hey, you, Bird—why don't you fly to the moon and retrieve your wits?" The man is pleased with himself when the customers laugh. He likes himself so much that he gives Uccello a *panino*, the ham hardened and curling where it protrudes from the roll.

On Via de' Tornabuoni, he encounters either a dream or a memory; he isn't sure which. At the Doney restaurant, he sees a line of military vehicles parked at the curb and, from limousines, important men debarking. What a lot of soldiers on patrol! Of course—for there's Il Duce himself, resplendent in ribbons, walking arm in arm with the beplumed and bemedaled Göring. The Führer, someone says, is already inside, seated at the table. There's a soldier with a machine gun, who says, *"Bambino, vai via* —shoo! Go home!"

He blinks his eyes and the soldier is gone. Il Duce has disappeared, if he was there at all. Göring, the traitor, has vanished. The men and women in front of Doney's—the cackling laughter, that nasal, indistinct speech—they're Americans. Uccello raises his fist. He hurls words across the street: "Garbage! Dogshit! Tourists!"

A dark blue car cruises past, its four occupants eyeing him narrowly. Carabinieri, heavy police, merciless. His mouth clicks shut. He hurries to the corner and darts down Via della Spada. At tiny Piazza di San Pancrazio, he sees the first cat, and on Via dei Federighi, he encounters three others, creeping in the shadows next to the wall. There's a powerful stench of catpiss.

It was once a palazzo, but now it's empty, stripped, a hulk of stone and brick. Boards cover the windows, timbers support the outside walls, and large signs proclaim DANGER, ENTRANCE FORBIDDEN. A fence of thick planks surrounds the ground floor, and above the fence a tilted catch-all extends over the street, to protect passersby from falling debris. Hundreds of cats make their home in the huge old house. Uccello has lived there since memory began.

He listens. Ears are better than eyes for sensing in the dark. The street is deserted. He steps in behind the timbers and runs his finger along the crack between two of the fence boards. He touches the match cover stuck there; no one has found his door. He urinates outside, adding his scent to that of the cats.

He pushes the bottom of the one plank, which swings inward on silent hinges, and slips through sideways. He closes the door and bolts it. Here the darkness is so thick he can feel it on his arms. His skin senses the great ruined doorway as an absence in the stone wall, and he steps through.

The cats make more noise than Uccello makes. He hears them moving over the floors above and in the far rooms of the ground floor. His natural tendency is upward, up the wide staircase to the topmost room, the room above the surrounding roofs, with windows opening in all four directions and all possible danger below him. But against his nature, he forces himself downward through the hole in the marble floor, into the cellar. Cats shift out of his path. He stops, extends his hand, and touches wood. He listens. Already the moaning has begun.

His room is off the cellar, actually outside the wall of the house, under the street. It's a round opening in an ancient foundation whose building no longer exists. It was a cistern perhaps, or an oubliette, and it has a low, round arch for a doorway. He himself made the wooden door to fit the opening. With the door closed, his body heats the space. With the door closed, he can't hear the old palazzo groaning, singing, and chuckling above him.

For now, he leaves the door open. He lights his candle and God shines forth on the brick wall, sunrays beaming around his head. In God's breast, where the heart is, stands the figure of the Son, also beaming light. Both Father and Son extend their arms to Uccello, inviting him into the curved wall to have some meat and a glass of wine, and to relate all that has happened to him during the day.

The cats, too wary to enter, crouch outside the door, their eyes yellow in the light. They protect him from rats, mice, and lesser moving creatures. They crouch in a semicircle just beyond the arch, the light caught in their eyes and whiskers. Uccello speaks frankly to the Father and Son, and they nod in unison. This is no news to them. They penetrate all disguises, know everything already, and have long been prepared for Hermann's reappearance. They convey to Uccello the necessity of betrayal, of evil as a principle that enhances good, and with one voice they give him his task. The cats, motionless, wait and watch. The old palazzo moans like a distant organ, a treble wailing above a sound so deep, so rooted, that it vibrates through the walls and into his bones.

He shuts his door, puts out the light, and lies down on the bed, a thin mattress on a pallet of boards. He covers himself with his tattered blanket. A question occurs to him: will Hermann, in one form or another, continue to reappear, to betray Il Duce over and over? But Father and Son have receded and there's no light, no answer. Still listening, he floats to sleep, rises from the earth, hovers cloud-borne and, toward dawn, falls like a feather to his bed again.

He sits up, sharply awake, then stands. On the stone arch of his doorway, he finds the smooth spot. From his pocket, he takes the clasp knife, its short blade worn thin over the years, and hones it further on the capstone. "Will this be sufficient for the day?" he asks, but he already knows the answer: with faith, anything would be sufficient, even just his hands.

The cellar is still pitch black, but the ground floor has light like a gray mold. Ahead of him, cat shapes retreat over piles of plaster, disappearing in the rubble. From the corner of the ceiling, a stone drops and strikes sparks off the marble floor. At the fence, he stops and listens, then unbolts the board and opens it a crack. There's no one. He slips out, drops the board into place, and replaces the match cover.

* * *

All morning he perches on the steps of the monument, in the rain. Foreigners in raincoats emerge from the hotel, their umbrellas pop open, and off they go to purchase the city with their money. Taxis arrive and depart. The doorman in his fancy uniform helps with luggage, performs like a monkey, grins, bows, and stuffs tips into his pockets. The April rain is cold—there's heaven's ice in it—and Uccello shivers, hunched over, his arms pressed to his sides. In his chest, the word glows like a glass ball.

Noon comes to the churches. The bells of Santa Maria Novella sound midday, then those of San Lorenzo behind him, and then the deep clangor from Santa Maria del Fiore, the Duomo. As noon rings all over town, the rain shuts off and the clouds break. Sunlight brushes the city. A blond, shining girl in a white dress steps forth from the Baglioni and catches a concentration of light. Watching her, astonished at her brilliance, he almost misses the dark bulk in the doorway behind her, swelling out and along the front of the hotel, then into Via de' Panzani.

He jumps to his feet, and stumbles. Has his body frozen? He can't straighten his back, his hips have locked in the roosting position, and there's no feeling in his feet. He stretches his arms and hobbles forward brokenly. Hermann has already vanished.

A command comes from within him: Fly! It pulsates rapidly and shoots flashes of heat and light. His hips crack, his hands and feet tingle, and the sky opens wide before him. He lifts his elbows as his legs carry him forward, and in no time at all the gray suit is close enough to touch. He could put his nose on the jiggling back! He could reach with one stroke the bristly rolls of fat above the collar. He clamps his mouth shut to hold back a shriek of triumph.

At the Caffè Gilli, the traitor finds a seat at a table under the awning, and the same obsequious waiter comes forward, rubbing his hands together, ducking and bowing. When Hermann speaks, his face is like the ravaged earth opening to reveal a burial pit.

Uccello continues by, circling the piazza and then alighting across the street from the café. The pavements have already dried and the sun is bright, the sky clear. Beneath the awning, Hermann, his jowls the color of raw meat, stares with tiny eyes at the passing streams of cars and people. Uccello could shout and attract his attention. Uccello could step right over there and insert the knife between him and his thoughts, where the neck joins the head.

While watching the one thing, he has missed another, and now he finds his view cut off by a blue shirt, dark blue tie, and, at eye level, a brass tie clip in the shape of a rifle. He glances up at the jutting chin, the underside raw from shaving. It's the same officer who arrested him yesterday, but afoot this time, and saying, "Do you know what I'll do if I catch you on this piazza again?"

"On my honor, sir—"

"I'll wring your neck like a chicken. Understood?"

It is understood. Uccello, scooting along the street, glances in at the café, where the waiter has just served Hermann a pink-and-green shrimp salad and a tall glass of beer.

He hurries around the block and enters the piazza from the loggia. From behind a column, he sees the officer not thirty feet away, but looking in the other direction. He backs off and hops around another block, but again there's the policeman, standing like a statue, jaw thrust forward, a pigeon circling his head.

Six streets feed into Piazza della Repubblica, and Uccello tries them all, and each time he sticks his nose in, he meets the officer. Worse, he has lost sight of Hermann behind the moving cars, the crowds of tourists. Has he finished his rich lunch? Escaped again? The policeman, the people, the traffic through the piazza: impediments in his path and perhaps a sign that God has changed his mind. Can God, having spoken, retract His word?

Uccello pauses, his faith shaken. In his chest, he feels only his rapidly knocking heart. What faith can one place in a heart?

Miraculously, then, the officer strolls into Via degli Strozzi and is gone. The way clears and the air brightens. People and cars turn thin and vanish in the flood of light. Without effort, Uccello glides across the piazza and in beneath the canopy.

He forgets to open his clasp knife, but God provides: there it is in his fist, already open. Does his hand drive the blade, or does the knife draw his hand? Hermann says, "Unk, unk, unk!" Then the blade does a perfect thing, it traces the arc of a circle. It disappears in the roll of fat at the base of Hermann's skull, and stays there.

Uccello flies from the screams, shouts, and exploding din.

Could that sound be a siren already, or is it the blood howling in his ears? He meets the young officer hurrying toward the piazza. At the center of a ball of light, Uccello streaks westward into Via della Spada.

Care is pointless, caution a luxury now. He sails along Via dei Federighi to his door in the fence. He kicks the plank inward and lets it fall shut behind him. Why lock it? He's in God's hands. He has performed his task. Cats scatter ahead of him. A rusty can clatters down the stairs. A clutch of mortar rattles on the floor.

In his room, the darkness weighs around him, and even with the door closed he hears the old house lamenting. Trembling, he lights the candle. There are only the walls of brick, like a tube on end, with himself at the bottom. Too shaky to stand, he sits on his pallet. "God?" he says.

Gradually, his pulse slows and his breathing returns to normal. Is it his ears singing, or does the palazzo suddenly resound with music? Past the candle, then, God looms up smiling, the Son smiling within his chest. Both Father and Son welcome him with their arms, and Uccello rises to be embraced.

* * *

A few days have passed. One evening, after shift, Sergeant Garbari and Officer Mulinaro leave the *questura* together. The sergeant says, "I wanted to speak to you because there's something I don't understand." They walk to Viale Spartaco Lavagnini, a broad boulevard, and stop in the open where no one will overhear.

"Now then, tell me," says the sergeant, "why did you shoot?"

"Everyone was shooting," the officer says.

"I know, but you fired first. You killed an unarmed man. I saw you, I was right there."

Officer Mulinaro lifts his chin. "Then you should have put it in your report."

"Perhaps I should have. You would've been sent for retraining, with a black mark on your record. The record lasts forever, determines your future, defines you for what you are. You would be known as one who can't control his weapon, who can be trusted only so far and no farther. While other men became lieutenants and captains, you would have found it hard to rise above sergeant. Should I have put such a mark in your record?"

"You should have told the truth," the officer insists.

"But I don't know the truth."

"That Uccello," says the officer, "he might have been unarmed, but he was guilty. He had murdered a man not two hours before."

"If that's why you killed him, I certainly should have reported you. It's not your function to determine guilt or innocence."

"But he was worthless, a nothing—trash. He murdered a well-to-do visitor to our city. Now justice has been done."

"I see, you think yourself to be the instrument of justice. How would you like that to appear in your record? It brings up the question of dismissal, not promotion—the question of whether you should be sent to the mental facility."

Officer Mulinaro says nothing. He looks at the sidewalk and shifts his feet. Sergeant Garbari says, "As for worthlessness, not one of us is worth very much, everything considered. Who is remembered, once dead? Only the great tyrant—the Hitler, the Stalin. The little tyrant, the Benito Mussolini, is laughed at and forgotten."

Officer Mulinaro straightens up and says, "All right, if you want the truth—I was frightened down in that cellar. It was dark with only those flashlights moving around. When the door opened and that shape came out, I didn't think—it was like some big bat. I pulled the trigger. I am ashamed of myself. That's what should go into my record."

The sergeant waits, but Officer Mulinaro has finished. He looks stricken and his eyes dart from side to side. The sergeant takes a deep breath, lets it out, and says, "Good, I was right, then. Shall we go?"

They walk back toward the station. The young man still hasn't understood. He says, "Will you alter your report?"

Sergeant Garbari laughs. "What, and look like a fool? No, the issue is closed."

They continue to where they parked their cars that morning. As they separate, Mulinaro says, "Do you mind if I ask a personal question? Why is it that, with all your years of service, you're still a sergeant?"

"Yes, I do mind," says the sergeant. "You should learn never to ask personal questions. You should do your duty, no more and no less." He pauses. "But I will say this: you remind me of myself when I was your age. Back then, I knew a lot more than I know now. Good night, Mulinaro."

What kind of answer was that? No answer at all. Mulinaro waits until the sergeant has gone, then he drives to the *viale* and joins the stream of traffic, heading home by his usual route.

Annunciation

The girl left her hotel and wandered through the streets until she no longer heard English spoken. It was only April, but she already had a golden tan, and as she walked, her golden hair swung and swayed over the shoulders of her new white dress. White heels, white purse; she was all in white, and what clear blue eyes, what a slim body, what a free and graceful stride! A heart-shaped golden locket, on a thin gold chain, gleamed between her breasts. Another golden chain disappeared into the high collar of her dress. Her heart itself perhaps hung from that one.

In late afternoon, in the lovely spring light, she emerged into an oddly formed piazza. She looked at her map. Ah, that church: Santa Maria Novella. There was Stairs Street, there Sun Street, and there the Street of Ditches, Via de' Fossi. At a newsstand, she saw a large headline displayed: UCCELLO UCCISO. She took her compact dictionary from her purse. Bird murdered? Simpleton killed?

Neither meaning seemed right for a headline. There were lots of things she didn't understand yet, but give her a month, she would learn. She had come straight to Florence from Los Angeles, the trip a present from her father, and already she loved this beautiful, old, famous city, Dante's city, Boccaccio's, and Michelangelo's. It was also Professor Phillip Whiteside's city.

At the center of the piazza, she sat on a stone bench and spread her skirt evenly on both sides. To a casual observer the houses might have seemed shabby and run down, but to her the signs of age bespoke authenticity. The Italian language, too, was ancient, going back to Latin, the mother tongue, and beyond that, in the darkness of prehistory, to the tongue spoken by Adam and Eve in Eden.

Even these pigeons, to judge by the thick streaks of lime on the front of the church, must have had quite an ancestry, and she could see why. It was mating season. Hundreds of males strutted, swelled their necks, spread their tails, and ruffled their feathers, and hundreds of females pretended not to notice. One of the females hopped onto the bench beside the girl, a chirring male close behind, and if she hadn't waved them away, they might have tried doing it in her lap.

From her purse she removed her new leather writing portfolio and her gold Mark Cross ballpoint pen. At the top of the first creamy sheet, she wrote, "Florence, Italy," and the date. She thought for a moment, then began.

Dear Professor Whiteside:

As you can see by the postmark, I am here in your city, the City of Flowers. By a curious paradox I feel closer to you here than ever I felt in Arcata, California. I have waited a long time before writing—so long that I don't even know if you are still teaching at Humboldt State, not to mention whether you remember me. But on the assumption that you are and do, I want to say that here among these stones, with the warm sunlight on the ancient houses, I feel, as I never did at the university,

that I can speak to you openly and without shame. Dear
Phillip, my thoughts are bursting forth like the flowers
of spring.

She paused. On the other benches were women, middle-aged to
old, talking animatedly, keeping an eye on their children and
grandchildren, who ran, played, shrieked, and squabbled. Off to
one side, a group of men argued passionately, waving their arms.
In a blue car parked by the news kiosk, four carabinieri smoked
and chatted. Young lovers and a few old down-and-outs lay on the
grass. A constant stream of people passed through the piazza, as
cars entering from three streets funneled into the Via de' Fossi.

I see now why you love Florence so. Of course, I'm
having trouble with the language—I didn't learn all I
should have in your class. I can't even remember which
words are masculine and which feminine. Are there
neuters? I wish you were here to answer my many questions. But already I understand Dante's wonderful poem
better than I did in the seminar. Remember where he
talks of the brown air? Well, the air in Florence really is
brown, though I guess it's more pollution than poetry.
Anyway, just imagine, on this very bench where I sit,
Dante Alighieri probably sat at some time in his life,
longing for his Beatrice.

The girl wrote swiftly, with deep concentration, filling the page
with sweetly rounded script. Around her flowed streams of citizens, language erupted and flowed around her, but she was lost in
the moment.

To become educated takes so very long, Phillip, and it
takes longer yet to grow up and learn who you are—I
mean who I am. When I graduated last spring, I still
didn't know. I went back to Los Angeles to work in my
father's business, and I took courses at UCLA to keep

my mind from dying. No courses in literature though, for this is the real world. I studied public relations, which my father requires in his business. He owns a ticket agency, so if you want to see the Rams, Raiders, Angels, Dodgers, and Lakers, let me know. I am an asset to the business, he says, and I suppose I am one. I help with parties and dinners for big sports stars, having replaced my mother in that respect, who got tired of the frenzy, the liquor, and the late nights that go with the job of being hostess. But that's another story.

This girl, this golden girl in white, how the men stared at her, and how the mothers and grandmothers gazed. Not one of the women could ever have been like this girl, so wealthy, unblemished, and radiant. The men were stricken with desire, the women stunned by awe, envy, fear. Even the pigeons kept an eye on her. When the sun sank behind the loggia, and the light suddenly softened, her hair retained a measure of brightness, prolonging the day.

You seemed so austere in that class, you were sarcastic, you gave off such waves of hatred it was frightening, especially to me, who had no background in literature or language. If you remember, I was a psychology major, scraping by, learning about the behavior of rats under stress. You did me the kindness not to call on me. I lived in fear that your see-all eyes, your voice as sharp as the executioner's sword, would select me for the day's demonstration. That Friday afternoon when I came to your office—I waited until no one would be around—did you know I came trembling to beg for a grade-change on my Paolo and Francesca paper? I was prepared to abase myself, weep floods of tears, submit to virtually any humiliation if only I could get a C for the course. To graduate I had to have a C.

Annunciation

She stopped and looked up. For some time, she had been aware of presences near her. Now she focused on the three young men who, bolder than the others in the piazza, stood together before her, looking her up and down. One of them had a cast on his left wrist, callused hands, sloping shoulders, and a bow in his back, as if he lifted stones for a living. The second looked soft and repulsive, his black hair slicked back, his teeth small and brown and crooked. The third, in tight jeans that made his sex prominent, had the arrogant unblinking stare, the cocky stance, and the curling, you-are-beneath-me mouth of the quarterback she'd had a crush on in high school.

She was no fool; she knew how to handle this type. It wasn't only in Italy, and not only recently, that she'd been besieged by men. You ignored the beasts and they lost heart, or you said sharply "No," or "Sit," and their courage fled. She looked through these three until they vanished.

Do you remember that afternoon? It might have been a small thing for you, but it was very large for me, virtually a revelation that I didn't know how to handle at the time. But now that I have matured and am well along on the road laid out for me by destiny, I want to speak out at last. Let me assure you, I write not to throw the past in your face and cause you pain, but purely to acknowledge my debt, for that afternoon, though you didn't know it, I received my education. No, I still don't understand the ins and outs of Dante's Heavenly Rose, with the saints clinging inside like a choir of aphids. I was not meant for intellectual pursuits. But coming across you drunk in your office that afternoon, the shock of it, set me on the path to understanding how joy rises from despair, light out of darkness. Oh, Phillip, if you will, let my light flash over to you this day.

The three young men had separated. The soft one was behind her, making a suggestive, slurping noise like a big dog licking his parts. To her left, Broken Wrist leered, and straight ahead Tight Pants rotated his pelvis and stared at her breasts. When the soft one came around in front, she gave them a look that said they were pigs at a trough.

I knocked at your door, then in fury wrenched the knob. For hours I'd waited, building my strength, only to find you absent. What a surprise when the door opened. "Get out, goddammit," you said, sitting there in the half-dark, your face all destroyed by vodka, bitterness, and tears. To this day I don't know why I didn't back away and run, unless I was meant not to, unless already I was on my destined path, which was meant to cross yours. It was as if someone shoved me in there, sat me in the chair, and said, "Listen." Oh, what these ears heard! You'd wasted your life, you said. You numbered your failures on your fingers. You were a sad case, you said, a bad example as husband, father, and lover. You had lost the distinction between right and wrong. You believed in nothing but vodka—vodka was God. You drank God from the bottle. Nothing could stop the tirade—you were on automatic. You flayed yourself before me. How you must have loathed yourself afterwards.

I said nothing. What did I know, psych major though I was? When you said, "Leave," I left. You were mumbling by then, passing out. Later, no great change occurred. You never mentioned it and were your old sarcastic self in class. On the final exam I couldn't respond to the intellectual questions and wrote instead a page about the love that drives the universe. You gave me a C and the rest is history. But now I want to say, must say, that your life was not wasted, no matter how you treated

your wife and children, no matter how far short you've
fallen as a scholar, no matter how much you drink—for
I am living proof of your success. I, because of you, am a
whole human being, ready to embrace my fate.

The greasy one, the pig-dog, sat on the bench to her left, while
Broken Paw sat to her right. Rooster stepped directly in front of
her. She glared at them. "Go away!" she said.

What I couldn't do for you then, I could do now. I have
grown almost unbelievably strong. I could take your
head, containing so much knowledge, so much pain, between my hands and release love's light into you, calming your frenzy, easing your bitterness. Phillip, I would
paint my eyes for you, decorate my body cunningly, and
dance. Forgive me, I didn't start out to say all this, but
now that it's written, it's true. May you walk in light. I
love you.

Anne Marie

Rooster stepped forward until his sex was right in her face. He
gyrated his hips. She closed the portfolio and tucked it and the
gold pen into her purse. She got up to leave.

That is, she tried getting up, but the two on both sides had their
hands on her skirt, pinning her to the bench. Rooster put his hand
on the back of her neck, under her hair, and began bending her
head toward his crotch.

With her fingers she got hold of one gold chain and pulled the
whistle free. She put it to her mouth and blew. The blast shrilled
off the church and around the piazza. Pigeons burst upward and
out in all directions. She screamed, "Rape!"

Carabinieri came running, pistols out, and other police appeared from the side streets. Cars halted. A crowd gathered. She
pointed at the three men and shouted, "You and you and you!"
The three stood frozen.

The sergeant in charge of the carabinieri spoke English. "Signorina, what happened?"

"Those beasts fouled me with their touch."

"You are injured?" He snapped his fingers and demanded to see her passport. "What is your hotel?"

"The Grand Hotel Baglioni."

"Go there," he said.

She arose from the bench, straightened her dress, and started off. The sergeant accompanied her as far as the kiosk. "Look," he said, pointing at the headline. "The police killed this Uccello today, right in the next street. Blood makes men nervous. Do not sound that whistle. Are you a woman? Do you know men? Then say no if you wish, and leave untouched." He backed off a step and saluted with his gloves.

She turned away and walked up a narrow street, toward the Baglioni. A pigeon from the piazza shot past her head so close she felt the wind in her hair. She shook her hair free and strode on.

Grace

First there was light and then there was dark. The light, very far away now, seemed only a glimmer in the surrounding darkness. It was as if someone on the other side of a broad river had struck a match. The Mississippi? The Nile? It could have been any river, he'd seen so many, or no river at all, and the light might not have been in his eye but in his head. "Mama?" he said, but there was so much noise—whines, howls, and static—that if she answered, he couldn't hear her voice.

On both sides, he felt the comfort of a bed. It was a hotel, that was it, and he remembered getting there on the train from Rome. From the station he'd gone to the Grand Hotel Baglioni, and on Borgo de' Greci, at a sculpture studio, he had ordered a marble boy and girl to play in the fountain in his courtyard. Lying still, he returned from nowhere gradually. Piece by piece, Florence reconstituted itself around him. It was past midnight and before dawn. He had been to a hospital to see Professor Whiteside. He had lost his taxi and then become lost himself in the maze of dark streets near the Arno. The Arno—that was the river! But what a mistake—his mother was nowhere near the Arno!

His mother lay in Denver, in the light. He himself lived in Marrakesh, where there was an absence in his fountain. This was the month of April, and a small man smelling of urine had been following him around, reading the newspaper over his shoulder, clinging like a burr while making furious, strangled sounds. For what purpose? He didn't yet know and might not know for years. But he could be sure of one thing: there was a purpose. All things had a reason. Though he rarely could see how, everything fit together. Not a bird but had its mission in the shifting arrangement, not a feather but sent back light. The blackest birds, crows, ravens, vultures, reflected the sunlight most brightly.

It was dark in his room. He knew the room was dark, because he'd drawn the drapes himself. So the flashing lights were in his head. They had reason to be there, since everything had a purpose. But if everything had a purpose, even his mistakes stood to reason, and therefore there was no such thing as a mistake. "Ha!" he said, and thought a dog had barked. Could there be a dog in bed with him? That whining in his ears; there might be a dog. Or perhaps someone had left a radio on and the station had gone off the air.

* * *

Warren Greenwald was fifty years old. He hadn't lived in the palace for forty-five years. The palace, in the hills above Denver, was occupied by his father and the new stepmother he'd never seen. His father, William Greenwald, still smoked four big cigars a day and, at age seventy-five, showed no sign of tapering off in any aspect of his life. He had already outlived two wives. He planned to give his third, named Bibi, a good run for his money.

When Warren's mother died, he was sent first to a Montessori school in Chicago, then to a military academy in Indiana, and then to a prep school in Upper New York State. Finally, he went to Yale, carried there by pinball money. His father manufactured pinball machines. He didn't try placing them in territories, for though big money lay in that side of the business, there also lurked strife. William Greenwald hadn't time for warfare. It was his mission to conceive of and manufacture the most dazzling pinball machines in America.

A genius in that respect, he was also very lucky with money. The economic riptides that drowned so many entrepreneurs always, for some reason, left him high and dry above the moil. In the 1950s therefore, when he first saw television, he had the cash to launch his ship. He envisioned televised pinball, and families vying for high scores in virtually every living room in the U.S.A. He built a laboratory behind the palace. He hired engineers, mathematicians, electronic wizards.

It wasn't that the ship sank, but that the voyage took longer than expected. He'd left America too far behind. But a decade and a half later, when America finally caught up, who was first on the market with a line of sophisticated video games? And who, while conventional minds were organizing video-game arcades in territories, made the quantum leap into the home computer industry? William Greenwald had always made money. But in the 1970s he made a continual killing. The 1980s saw the slaughter in full spate.

It was at Yale that Warren Greenwald realized how different he was from the young men and women around him. They astonished him; he wouldn't have thought of behaving as they did. To understand them, he had to study them as if they were a different species. He observed their behavior. He took notes. He tried thinking through to the principles. One impulse that they seemed to have in common was desire. Desire was their governor.

They wanted good grades in their courses, and so they studied. From a desire for health, they exercised and ate properly and got lots of sleep—except when they desired wild fun. Then they spent weekends drinking, hardly sleeping at all, and afterward, to regain their health, they slept more and worked harder than ever. Most peculiar of all, they desired each other. They would scheme deviously, make labyrinthine plans, just to couple, copulate, and make arrangements to meet again. Whatever present they might be in, they desired something ahead of them, as yet unattained. Their actions were predicated upon a future.

He looked to his own experience for comparison, but he found nothing to measure by. What was their feeling? One term, he'd taken a course by mistake—he'd written in the wrong code number—and, once in the classroom, he'd seen no reason not to stay. It was a course on the Greek conception of the good. The professor, named Whiteside, riveted Warren's attention. His voice was so deep and expressive, his diction so precise, and his face so perfectly proportioned that he seemed to personify knowledge itself. Warren couldn't take his eyes off him in class. He was profoundly moved. But was this desire? Was it predicated on a future? As stirred as he was while in class, he didn't look forward to it, he didn't always attend, and he didn't look beyond the class toward something that might happen because of it. Still, it was the only course he took at Yale for which he received a grade higher than C. He got a B—.

At Yale no substantial donor's son is dismissed without compelling reasons. Warren's grades seemed compelling, but might there not be mitigating circumstances? He was invited to the counseling center for an interview. He was given tests. He became something of a celebrity among the psychologists, who considered it a miracle, almost proof of God's existence, that one so alienated could pass any course in the curriculum. The center made a plea on his behalf. Grades or no, could he be allowed to stay on, for scientific purposes? In the interests of science, the administration acceded, extending his period of probation to allow two psychologists to write him up in professional papers, one on anomie, the other on autism.

Though not yet a sophomore, he left college when his class graduated. He was twenty-one years old and financially independent. William Greenwald's second fatherly act—the first having been to lie with Warren's mother—was the creation of a trust fund for the boy's maintenance. Warren had only to let the bank in Denver know his address to receive a large monthly check. When he forgot to let the bank know, his checks accumulated, so sometimes he received a pile of money.

He wandered down the East Coast to Florida, either hitchhiking or renting a car, and then he wandered back North through New Haven, to Boston. In Scollay Square, he met the woman who gave him his first sexual experience with another person. She was the first woman who had asked him. Of the two possible responses, he chose the second. "Yes," he said.

She hooked her arm through his and led him along dingy streets to an apartment. Then she said, "Honey, I'm sick, you know?" She introduced him to her daughter Cindy, a thin child of ten. He hesitated not because of the child's age or the marked smell of garbage in the living room, but because he hadn't the slightest idea of what came next. No matter. Cindy showed him and he was amazed.

He sent that address to the bank in Denver. He might well have remained forever in his new nuclear family, but one day, while the mother was out, her social worker paid a call. Warren answered her questions to the best of his ability, and when Cindy tried clapping a hand over his mouth, he pulled her playfully onto his lap. The family nucleus exploded.

Warren wandered westward, making generous swings to the north and south. Traveling by bus, train, plane, sleeping outdoors sometimes, sometimes putting up in grand hotels, he saw what America had to offer. From the Gulf to the Canadian border, through swamps, woods, plains, and passes, he stored his mind with pictures. He took his time. He had no desire to be other than where he was, who he was. It rained, the sun shone, a wind whipped up, a blizzard buried the roads, or he baked. Coming to Denver by accident, he saw the stately bank where his trust fund reposed. He saw his father's house on the hill, behind a barred gate. He went to a cemetery to think about his mother.

At Los Angeles, America ended. He looped north along Interstate 5, and America ended again in San Francisco. From time to time, he tried practicing what Cindy had taught him, but other children hadn't her knowledge, and when he succeeded, it was only because he was bigger and stronger. When at Seattle he once more came to the end of America, he turned east and kept going until he heard French spoken. He liked the sound of French. He thought he was in Canada, but he must have slept through part of the trip, for this was Paris. He stayed for quite a long time.

By age thirty, he had established his lifelong pattern of finding a good hotel, eating in good restaurants, and following where his senses led him. They led him to museums, brothels, cathedrals, fish markets, mosques, and bazaars. He discovered Cairo, Tangier, and Marrakesh. He found in North Africa no limit to what his money would purchase, and so he bought and bought. From among the boys and girls, he bought those not requiring gentle treatment, and he got his money's worth. He bought a house in Marrakesh, and stayed.

In Tangier he received more than he'd paid for. It was a small disturbance, which went away. A year later it returned, but then subsided. From time to time, it made demands, and when he finally flew to Paris to consult a doctor, it was firmly entrenched. Medicines killed off the foliage, but it lived in the root and kept sending out fresh shoots. An ulcer left a lesion on his left side, and another showed up in the back muscle near the spine. He gained weight. His eyesight blurred. On his face, certain signs appeared —a redness, puffiness, and those vertical ravines descending from his eyes, nose, and mouth.

Whenever he went to Paris, his doctor shook his head and increased the dosage. But Warren already had that characteristic gait, as if he were climbing stairs. His doctor said, *"Sacrebleu,* this is the grandfather and grandmother of all love diseases!"

On his travels, he picked up pretty paintings, statues, and vases, to adorn his home. The pretty girls and boys grew up, or rarely didn't, and he replaced them from the endless supply. While sitting in his courtyard one day, watching the tree-shaped fountain of water, he noticed that the water was always moving, yet the shape remained still. Instantly, he grasped the principle: as with the fountain, so with his life. He saw what was lacking—two statues holding hands behind the trunk of water, the water like leaves forever showering on their heads, the light falling, altering hour by hour, upon two wet, laughing, unchangeable marble children.

He knew just where to buy what he desired. He called to be driven to the airport. He rented a plane and had himself flown northeast to Rome. The disease hummed, buzzed in his head like wasps, and on the train he was attacked by a fierce electrical storm, booming with thunder, with lightning darting from black clouds. But in Florence the streets were dry. He had himself driven to a studio on Borgo de' Greci, where he explained what he wanted. The sculptor would do some studies. Then Warren could choose.

He spent a week at the Baglioni, waiting. He took dinner in the hotel and lunch at the Caffè Gilli, in Piazza della Repubblica. The days were warm, the sky clear, and streams of people afoot or in cars flowed through the piazza. Pigeons foraged under the café's awning, and now and then he dropped some crumbs, to see them gather and become so excited that they hopped up onto the tables. Then the waiters, clapping their hands, waving napkins, would chase them off.

He first noticed the little man at the center of some disturbance on the sidewalk by the café. In fact, he was causing the disturbance. He had grabbed hold of a street sign and was shaking it back and forth, shouting at the top of his voice, while nearby another man, well dressed, complained to a policeman. The po-

liceman then wrenched the little man off the signpost and took
him away.

Warren ate lunch. A procession of noisy Germans filed in and
settled at a long table to his right, and there in the middle of the
line was the same man: broken shoes, ragged pants, gray stubble
on his chin. The man stopped and let the tourists go, then yelled
something at Warren. Bubbles of spit formed on his lips. His sharp
blue eyes, set too close together, gave the look of insanity. A
waiter waved a napkin at him and said, "Begone."

Warren paid his bill and, on the way to his hotel, stopped to
pick up a newspaper. The man, his chin practically on Warren's
sleeve, gave off the stench of urine, but it was stronger than urine,
a fox smell, the smell of a lion cage in a zoo.

Though Warren knew no Italian, he'd spent enough time in
Italy to get the gist of the news. He recognized the words for
crime and violence. Florence was becoming more like New York,
Chicago, and Los Angeles. Then a name leaped out, Professor
Phillip Whiteside, *ferito gravemente,* in the *Ospedale di San Gio-
vanni in Borg'Ognissanti.* His old professor here? Gravely hurt?

The years dropped away and he heard that strong voice, saw
the beautifully proportioned face. It was suddenly as if the earth
had split, a chasm had opened—on the one side *what was,* on the
other *what is.* It was such a deep chasm, and so long and wide,
that there was no possible way back across. A groan welled up in
his throat.

He'd gotten to his hotel. He took the elevator to his room on
the top floor. From his window overlooking the Piazza dell'Unità
Italiana, he saw, squatting on the steps of the monument, the
same little man. He was staring up, straight at Warren's window.
"Who sent you?" he said, his voice breaking.

His legs were trembling. He pulled the drape and sat on the
bed. His hands shook. *Then* he had loved the professor; *now* an
evil little man was stalking him. Between then and now lay the
whole of his adult life, confused, a shambles.

The disease racketed in the room. Water pipes banged and someone dumped a load of copper kettles. A thousand shards of mirror reflected the African sunlight. He lay back, depleted. He shut his eyes and put his hands over his ears. The whole of Africa was in his head, the wind howling, the sun beating on rocks and sand.

All things, then, did *not* fit perfectly. This did not fit. There *were* mistakes, after all, and he had made them—countless mistakes, overlapping like fish scales. Wherever he looked at his fish-shaped life, he looked at error.

The ringing he'd heard off and on turned out to be the telephone. "Who?" he said.

"Signor Giachetti will come tomorrow at four-thirty in the afternoon, to show his drawings."

Another mistake. Warren groaned.

At some point, he realized that the drapes were black. He got up and aimed for the window. Though it was dark outside, he could still see the hunched shape against the lighter stone of the monument. Perhaps he had fallen asleep. It made no difference whether he had or hadn't, for Warren would leave regardless.

He went down to the lobby and asked the clerk to call a taxi. The clerk raised his eyebrows, then nodded toward the door, where a cab already stood waiting. Warren eased through to the outside, got into the backseat, and said, "Hospital, *ospedale*—the San Giovanni one."

The cab sped through the streets. Lights flashed by. A cat screamed in the front seat, or maybe it was a siren behind them.

At the hospital, he gave the driver fifty thousand lire. "Wait for me. Wait—understand?"

"Uet?" the driver said.

Warren got out. At the desk in the lobby, he asked for Professor Whiteside. The nun on duty unleashed a stream of Italian. Seeing that he didn't understand, she pointed to the clock and said, "No, no, no."

On the desk stood an alms box. The sign said I POVERI. Warren opened his wallet, withdrew one hundred thousand lire, and pointed to the box. The nun quickly put the banknote into the slot, glanced both ways, then wrote "307" on a slip of paper. Warren stepped to the elevator.

On a table beside the bed, an electric candle burned. There was only the one bed in the room, and above it was a frame from which the professor's leg hung suspended. The leg, in a cast from hip to ankle, looked enormous in the dim light. The left arm had a cast, too, and the right arm lay on top of the covers, the long fingers relaxed. He wore a cap of bandages. One eye was bandaged. The good eye, the left one, was closed.

When Warren sat down beside the bed, the chair scraped. The eye opened. "Professor," he said, "I am Warren Greenwald. I was in a class of yours once. I am sorry this happened to you. It should have happened to me instead."

The eye blinked.

"Do you remember?" Warren asked. " 'What is it that the lover of the good desires? He desires to make the good his own.' You read that to us, from Plato. It was beautiful. I have come to thank you for it. I was careless back then, but now I can make amends—at least to a small extent. Is there something I can do for you? If it wouldn't offend you, I would like to pay for your expenses here. Please let me. I have money. That's all I have."

The eye blinked again, and the lips parted. The professor tried to speak, but his jaws were wired shut. He said, "Oozh, oozh."

"Wait—be calm. It makes no difference. You don't have to say a word. Rest. I want to tell you about my life."

Professor Whiteside's eye darted to the left, then to the right, and again he tried speaking, but only a kind of whimper came out. Warren said, "I have not made the good my own, sir. I am ashamed of myself. I have not been a good man. I have lived in sin, without caring, without a thought, and I've hurt people who meant me no harm—innocent children even, yes, children. I have a horrible disease and I'm dying."

There, he had put it into words. His heart stirred and he closed his eyes. His heart grew large, swelled upward, and blocked his throat. Not since he was little had he experienced such pressure in his chest. He opened his eyes and tears gushed forth, running in hot streams down his cheeks. "Oh," he said, "oh, oh, oh." He fell forward onto his knees. He grabbed the limp hand and pulled it to his mouth. "I'm sorry, sorry, sorry. Forgive me." He kissed the hand, his tears wet it, he clutched it hard. He sobbed and choked. He howled out, "Have mercy! Have mercy!"

The hand twitched and jerked, trying to escape. Warren released it, horrified. What had he done? He'd fouled the professor with his touch. He'd wiped his face with the professor's hand—he'd slobbered all over it. The eye was wide and wild, and the mouth said, "Oooozh!" bubbling with saliva.

"Oh, forgive me," Warren said. He got up, turned, and stumbled out. He stumbled down the flights of stairs and burst into the lobby. The nun stared, then put up her hands to protect herself. Warren pushed on past, through the door and out. His taxi was gone.

He wandered in a maze of streets, totally lost. He had no idea where his hotel was, and every street he took, some no wider than alleys, bent around and brought him to the same tiny piazza. The houses stood high and dark above the narrow streets. He heard the hiss of his own breathing. Passing a ruined, boarded-up old palace, he smelled cats' urine and remembered the little man. He saw three, five, seven cats slinking in the shadow of the wall. So, it had been settled. He'd forfeited.

By accident he found the Piazza dell'Unità Italiana. He'd circled around to the opposite side of it. Entering from a crevice of a street, he made for the monument, walking slowly, deliberately close to it. The man wasn't there.

* * *

He awakened late the next morning. He had slept well. Without having to wrestle with hallucinations, he had fallen straight to sleep, and for once he hadn't dreamed. He felt lighter, refreshed, purified. In the mirror, his face seemed less puffy, and some of the flush had drained from his cheeks. After he shaved, he patted on an astringent lotion that drew his skin tight. It smelled of lime flowers. His head was silent. He dressed carefully.

When he left the hotel, he didn't glance at the monument. It no longer made any difference whether the man was there or not. Balanced, at ease, he strolled to the Caffè Gilli and took a table by the aisle. When the waiter approached, he ordered a shrimp salad and beer. He even felt hungry.

What a pretty day! The sun was out again, pedestrians were out in force, cars were moving through the piazza, and pigeons flew lazily, or pecked in the cracks between the paving stones. Ah, there was the stalwart young policeman from yesterday, bending slightly at the waist, giving directions to a tourist.

His salad and beer arrived. He took a forkful of shrimp and noticed that the policeman was now admonishing the little man, shaking a finger at him. The little man shrank back, like a frightened cat, and then slunk away. Warren wasn't surprised to see him. In the nature of things, he'd had to reappear, especially on such a seemly day, so perfectly arranged, with the sun bright in the sky, the buildings sharply defined around the piazza. His eyesight must have improved. There weren't those fuzzy outlines he'd grown accustomed to. It was as if a clouded glass had been removed, and all the shapes and colors sprang keenly forth.

To the right, there—look at that: that bump on the side of one of the loggia's columns! The little man's head, or half of it—one ear, a fierce eye. But a few steps away stood the policeman, hands behind his back. The head withdrew.

Warren, in no rush, took his time over the food. When the little man appeared in the next street to the left, he smiled, for the officer had moved, too, and was again blocking the way. How frustrated the little fellow must feel!

It happened twice more, as if directed and performed. Both the little man and the officer were circling the piazza counterclockwise, the officer strolling slowly, the little man scurrying around a whole block in order to enter from another street. Each time he entered, there was the officer. Warren smiled broadly.

But then Warren lost him. The officer changed directions and casually left the piazza. Warren put his fork down. His throat felt dry. He lifted his glass and drank a few swallows of beer. As he set the glass down, he remembered something: his professor had been named Arthur, not Phillip. He'd been middle-aged thirty-two years ago. In all probability, he was dead by now.

Warren laughed aloud. He'd poured out his soul to the wrong Whiteside. What a mistake! The waiter stopped and said, "Signore?" Warren reached for his wallet.

From the left, then, he saw the little man coming. He saw the knife. The blows to his back didn't hurt—they were more like nudges than stabs. He caught a whiff of cat urine. Then his head burst into brilliance, pure light without a shadow. It was all of a piece! All there was! And it stayed!

Two Paces East

When Phillip Whiteside returned to his apartment that morning, he found the door ajar. "Oh oh," he said. The lock had been ripped from the wood, and there were pry marks on the stone casing. A robbery. Very interesting. Interesting, but not crucial, for what could thieves have taken that he couldn't do without? Traveler's checks could be replaced. He carried his passport and cash on his person. He'd left maybe 150 dollars' worth of Swiss francs in a drawer up there, but that was nothing. His clothing, books, even his typewriter: there was nothing in the apartment that couldn't be replaced.

He stood on the landing for a bit, catching his breath. The climb from the lobby always winded him, and then, beyond this door were two more flights, ninety-nine steps in all, to the top level of the *soffitta,* the garret, that he'd leased for a year. He had chanced upon this apartment, and had lived there for a month before he thought to count the stairs, and then how fitting he found it, for Dante's *Commedia* had ninety-nine cantos, plus one at the beginning, to make a symbolic one hundred. Whiteside had come to Florence to write a monograph on one of Dante's major metaphors, the struggle upward toward perfection. Every time he climbed the stairs, therefore, he performed a small symbolic act. It pleased him to regard his essay as the hundredth step, a closure both literal and figurative, an expression of the *Commedia*'s perfection and, at the same time, the rounding into form of his own thoughts. Somewhat self-deprecatingly, in fact, he conceived of it as a three-part correspondence: as in God's creation, so in Dante's *Commedia*, and as in the *Commedia*, so in "The Figure of Ascent and Descent in Dante," which was the provisional title of his manuscript.

He pulled the door the rest of the way open and listened. Not a sound. The *malviventi*, the bad livers, had come and gone. He went up the narrow stone stairs to the bedroom. What a mess! They'd scattered his clothing on the floor, torn the bed apart, ransacked the storage closet. The drawer to the nightstand was open, of course, and the Swiss francs had vanished. One of his suitcases was missing. His travel clock was gone.

Up, then, to the top floor, to the dining room, kitchen, and bath. He used the dining room for a study, working at the table, sometimes reading on the cot that he'd brought in as an amenity, since there were only straight chairs in the apartment. The cot had been turned upside down and the mattress, on the floor, halfway under the table, had been adorned with a coil of excrement. He clenched his teeth. From the kitchen, he brought a wad of paper towels to scoop the thing up with, then he flushed it down the toilet. He removed the mattress pad and poured disinfectant on the ticking. He put the pad in the garbage. He threw open the windows and shutters for fresh air, then righted the cot and put the mattress on it.

He noticed that the doors to the credenza were open, but the significance didn't strike him right away. His typewriter and lamp were on the table, and his books—well, the books were gone. His traveler's checks remained. Then it hit him. Where was his manuscript? God, where were his notes? A lifetime of casual thought, then two years of specific preparation, plus the pages he'd written over the past two months of daily labor at that table: disappeared!

He hurried down the two flights to the landing and rang Signora Luzzi's doorbell. He waited, then rang again. Finally, he heard the bolts snap back, and then her door opened. He said, "Excuse me, signora, but I've been robbed. Would you call the police?"

She hesitated, then said, *"Sì, venga."* He stepped inside. She was wearing a blue robe and slippers, and her hair was tousled. "Did I wake you?" he said. "I'm sorry."

"It's not important," she said. At the hall stand, she dialed a number, then gave a rapid explanation. A voice crackled in the receiver. She rolled her eyes at Whiteside. "The police say to call the carabinieri."

As she was dialing again, a man's voice came from a room off the hallway. *"Cosa succede, Lena?"* She paused and called out, *"Niente,* never mind." Again she spoke into the phone, then listened. She asked Whiteside if anyone had been hurt. He shook his head. "No, no one was killed," she said. "Yes, I see."

She hung up. She gave Whiteside a sympathetic shrug. "You must go to the carabinieri," she said, "around the corner in Borg'Ognissanti."

"Thank you," he said. "I'm sorry I disturbed you."

"It's no great tragedy," she said. She let him out and bolted the door behind him. His last glimpse was of a bare, packed calf below her robe, and the furry blue pom-pom on her slipper.

* * *

At carabinieri headquarters, he got no farther than the entrance. He spoke to the duty officer there, through a slit in the bullet-proof window. The officer waved him away. "You are American. Go to the consulate on Lungarno Vespucci. They will write a letter, and we will investigate."

Whiteside nodded. He continued along Borg'Ognissanti for a block and then cut over to walk by the river. Though it was late November, there hadn't been enough rain yet to bring the water up. Today the air felt warm and moist, and there was a thick overcast. It was trying to rain, but couldn't. The back of his neck felt tense.

He entered the consulate between guards armed with machine guns. Inside, he stepped through the frame of a metal detector and presented his passport to another guard, who pointed him toward a door of bullet-proof glass. It led to a lobby. At the receptionist's window, he explained why he was there. The receptionist gave him a numbered card and told him to wait. Ahead of him were six people with similar cards, one of them a girl whose face was swollen from weeping. She held her hands clenched in her lap.

The moment he sat down, his number was called. Another heavy door, another lock. This one clicked as he reached for the handle, and he entered a room with a long counter, behind it several clerks whose job, apparently, was to stare. At least they stared at him, and then ignored him completely. No one came forward to help him. There were no other supplicants in the room.

Finally, he said, "Hey!" One of the clerks, a young man in glasses, sauntered over. Whiteside explained that he'd been robbed and that the carabinieri had sent him here for a letter.

"You should call the *polizia,* in Via Zara," said the clerk. "In any case, we don't write such letters."

"I did call the *polizia*. They're the ones who sent me to the carabinieri."

"Why would the carabinieri be involved? Was there a murder? Political violence? Perhaps drugs?"

"No, I lost a little money, not much. I lost my research, my notes, my manuscript. And the thief, or one of the thieves, took a crap on my bed."

"Ah, vandalism! See, you should have called the *polizia*. They handle cases of vandalism."

Whiteside turned and walked out. Halfway across the lobby, he noticed the girl still sitting there. On impulse, he knelt beside her and asked if he could help. She burst into tears at once, and between sobs poured out an incoherent tale about a friend of hers, in a hospital in Pisa. Something about trouble with doctors and police. Trouble getting in to see the consul.

Whiteside said, "This is the bureaucracy. It's like glue. Do you have any important friends in America? If so, or even if they're not important, have them get in touch with a congressman. Raise hell. Meanwhile, my name is Whiteside. I'm a professor here on leave. If there's anything I can do to help, stop by." He jotted his name and address on a piece of paper, then patted her hand.

On his way home, he stopped at the bookstore in Piazza Carlo Goldoni. The owner, Alessandro Delangelo, had been born in America but had become an Italian citizen. He specialized in books in English. Better yet for Whiteside's purposes, he seemed interested in talking about literature. He knew a lot, too. He and Whiteside had had lunch together twice, and Whiteside had told him about his paper.

Today he seemed dispirited, unless the mote was in Whiteside's eye. He did look pale, though. Whiteside told him about the robbery, then said, "They didn't take my money, they took my life."

"How can you joke?" Delangelo said. "What now?"

"What is there to do? I have ten months left in Florence. As I see it, I can either do nothing, or start over."

"But your notes. How can you start over without your research?"

"From scratch," Whiteside said. "I've come to buy the Singleton Dante. Who knows, without my notes, it might be better. At least it'll be different."

"You don't seem too upset," Delangelo said. "In fact, you seem almost relieved. Weren't you happy with what you'd done?"

"Let's put it this way. It isn't a tragedy to have to begin again. Since I can't proceed mechanically according to my outline, maybe I'll get more imagination into it. It's possible, you know. Anything is possible."

"Not anything," Delangelo said. "But I'm glad you're not destroyed by the loss. You'd better put heavy locks on your door. Florence is getting more and more like Chicago and New York."

"What about lunch this Friday? Could you make it?"

"This Friday, no. I have a doctor's appointment. Perhaps next week."

"I'll stop by," Whiteside said. "Take care of yourself. You look a little peaked." He bought the six-volume *Divine Comedy,* three books of text, three of commentary. It was a bilingual edition, the standard edition in English. His notes might have vanished, but his mind hadn't. His mind and these books were all he would need, since he'd been granted the gift of time. Time was truly of the essence.

* * *

His door now had two flat steel bolts that shot three inches into the stone wall. The locksmith who installed them said, "Guaranteed." But Whiteside, as he paid him, thought, What if the locksmith himself wants in? He couldn't help being suspicious. Signora Luzzi entertained male guests, some of them not too savory, from what he'd seen of them—and she might have mentioned that a rich American professor lived upstairs. She seemed friendly enough, neighborly, but who could tell? He knew almost nothing about her.

He knew, though, that she was acquainted with Signor Pulci, the rental agent through whom he'd gotten the apartment, and that there was no love lost between them. Just after Pulci had shown him the apartment and he'd taken it, they'd met Signora Luzzi on the stairs. She said, "The spider catches another fly, I see." Pulci said, "Please, he speaks Italian." She turned to White-side. *"Guarda bene*—watch out!"

Pulci said, "Whore! Signore, ask her what happened to her husband. Ask this virtuous widow what she did to him."

"Idiot, monster, Sicilian," she said, and went up to the next landing. "Ignoramus!" she called back.

It could have been Pulci who put the thieves on to him. To anyone who didn't know, he would seem rich. After all, he was living jobless in Florence, far away from California, and Pulci had seen him paying the year's rent in advance. How was he to know that the money came from savings, that his monthly stipend was about equal to a bank clerk's salary in Florence? He shopped frugally at the greengrocer's, the baker's. At the *salumeria* he bought a few ounces of ham and cheese. He read the newspaper only every other day and very seldom had more than one drink in the bar on Piazza Santa Maria Novella. He ate out every evening, but cheaply, at a trattoria or self-serve restaurant. It was his one full meal. The rest of the day, he snacked at home.

Even so, he got to know people. He tried practicing the language whenever possible, with the result that any of a dozen people could have marked him. Right across Via de' Fossi from his apartment was a garage where men perpetually loitered, talking, watching the women pass by. They didn't miss much that happened in the street. They knew when he left, when he returned. Some of them, out of envy, could have slipped upstairs and evened the score with the rich American.

Was he reasonably mistrustful, or had he grown paranoid? With a shock, he discovered that the bars over his dining-room window, from which he had a fine view over the roofs to Bellosguardo across the Arno, were only ornamental. He easily removed one of them, using just his hands. Any roof rat could do the same, break the window, and be inside in less than a minute. The shutter latch was a flimsy thing.

He bought a carpenter's hammer and kept it on the nightstand.

He bought a new alarm clock. He bought a mattress pad for the cot, though he needn't have, for he couldn't use it; the smell of disinfectant stayed in the mattress, reminding him of the other smell. He brought the study lamp to the bedroom, at first to read by, and then to write by. He took to working in the bed mornings, leaning against the headboard, a notebook on his knees. When he went up to the bathroom at night, he carried the hammer along.

But never in his life had he felt so fine. His morning hours simply melted as he worked, and when he was out shopping, or reading the newspaper in the piazza, or off on one of his long walks, his mind leaped to new connections. In the new form, his essay might not have been as methodical, but it lived a muscular life. From the moment when Dante the pilgrim tries ascending the Holy Hill by the easy way, but can't because a leopard, a lion, and a she-wolf prevent him; from the moment when his guide, the poet Virgil, appears, sent by God to lead him on the descent through hell; the whole pattern of ascents and descents sprang into being. The leopard: the pleasures of the senses. Lion: ambition. She-wolf: avarice. To climb up the Holy Hill is impossible until the pilgrim has somehow mastered those beasts that destroy men's souls. Without God's grace raining down from above, no man could ascend to bliss.

One afternoon, Whiteside came across Signor Pulci in the piazza. The agent said, "I hear you had some bad luck. *Terribile, è una tragedia.*"

"Sometimes a tragedy is a blessing in disguise," Whiteside said. "But how did you find out about it—through Signora Luzzi?"

"That one—what a beast. No, I heard the rumor in the stones, the way news travels in the quarter."

Whiteside laughed. "The stones, I see." The agent took on a gloomy expression and turned away.

* * *

The rains made a steady, drumming sound on the roof, but in a high wind, things rattled, thumped, and scraped out there. On a morning not long before Christmas, his doorbell rang. He pulled on his trousers and went down to the door. He carried the hammer. He didn't press the buttons that unlocked the street door and security gate, but waited, his eye to the peephole. Let whoever it was think he was out. Let them ring the bell for another tenant, gain access to the building, and come up to pry at his door again. He smacked the flat of the hammer against his palm.

But no one appeared. After a while, he gave up and started toward the bedroom. The bell sounded again. He tiptoed down to the peephole. Hell, it was Signora Luzzi. He drew the bolts.

"I'm sorry to disturb you, but my television isn't working. I think it's the antenna. May I?"

"Of course," he said. "Come in." He stepped back and she preceded him up the stairs. She was in her morning dress, the blue robe and slippers—the Virgin's color, he thought, and smiled. The Virgin wouldn't have had a leg like the signora's on her, or earned her living as the signora did. The signora, below the waist, seemed all muscle; she rippled as she climbed.

At the landing, she glanced into the bedroom and laughed. "Books in bed! What a monk you are. And that hammer—is it to protect yourself against me?"

He set the hammer down and followed her up to the dining room, where she opened the window and shutters, removed one of the bars, and leaned out. "Broken completely," she said. "I'll have to bring a *tecnico*. Will you be at home?"

"I'm here every morning."

"Tomorrow, then. Good. But please, don't hit him with your hammer."

"Then tell him not to use a pry bar on my door."

She gave him a slow look, then laughed. "I like you," she said. "Would you come to my house next Sunday, for dinner?"

"Why, I . . . Well, yes, thank you."

"At two o'clock. *Arrivederci.*"

"*Arrivederla,*" he said.

* * *

On Christmas Day, a Saturday, he felt disconnected, out of sorts. He'd gone to midnight mass the night before at the Duomo, had stood among some ten thousand others, and had heard almost nothing of the service. The public address system was faulty. Even the choral music hadn't the power to maintain coherent melody; it broke around the huge columns, flitted intermittently, like ghosts, in the high vaulting, and rained in fragments upon the congregation. The pipe organ, which should have boomed some stability into the chorus, instead gave off feeble, trickling sounds. Afterward, he walked home through a cold, damp fog.

It was the mass, he supposed, that spawned his Christmas morning dream. In the dream, he was recovering, had recovered with marvelous alacrity from an operation on his colon. The hospital released him in time for the Contessa's party, at her villa high on a hill in Fiesole. It was a sunny afternoon, very pleasant. On the terrace, men and women were dancing. There was light music. The guests could choose from a buffet of meats, seafood, and elaborate salads. He stood at the railing and looked out over the Arno Valley to the rolling hills of the Chianti, to the south. Beside him at the railing, the Contessa, a blue-eyed woman with tawny hair, said, "Don't be self-conscious, we are very patient— we can wait forever." She pointed down toward Florence. "See the Duomo there? It has waited for centuries."

At that moment, her husband appeared, a dark man in a black suit, with a strip of white shirt showing above his jacket collar. He took Whiteside's arm. "We want you to feel at home here. Please, have a drink." He held out a tray. Whiteside took the thimble-sized glass and drank down the dark liquid. The Contessa patted his arm. "There now," she said.

They led him between them to the buffet. The host said, "Try some of this." He extended a small plate with a lump of meat on it, a meat unfamiliar to Whiteside. It was conical in shape, like the heart of some small beast, yet flat on the base. An organ meat of some kind, was it? It was covered with an iridescent membrane, but was raw on the bottom where it had been severed.

Whiteside took it into his mouth and at once knew that he shouldn't have. It had a soft, mealy texture. But the Contessa and her husband were watching intently. He chewed, then swallowed. The Contessa smiled, and said, "Lucky for you they got it all, because—"

"It was cancer," the host said.

Whiteside awakened grimacing. "Ech," he said. He went up-stairs and brushed his teeth. He made coffee. But he didn't write that day because the fumes from the dream drifted between him and his notebook.

Nor did he write Sunday morning. He went for a walk instead. Happening by Delangelo's bookshop, he glanced in and saw the man at his desk in the rear. He tapped the window with his keys. Delangelo glanced up, then came tiredly to the door and let him in. His appearance was a shock to Whiteside. He couldn't help himself. He said, "Are you ill?"

"So it seems, and so it is. For once, appearance and reality are one and the same. That book you ordered finally arrived. I sent one of the girls around with it, but you weren't at home. Would you like some tea?"

"No thank you. What book was it? I don't remember."

"Sit down—I'll get it." He went into the back room. He re-turned, saying, "I'll give you a special price on it. It's used, now. I read it. Interesting."

Whiteside remembered. The book, *Wholeness and the Implicate Order,* by David Bohm, had caused a stir some years ago. White-side had meant to read it, but his intention got lost in a welter of intentions. The title surfaced again, in the *Times Literary Supplement,* not long after he'd come to Florence. So he'd ordered it and then forgotten once more. He said, "It seems I'm destined to read this—it keeps crossing my path. What did you think of it?"

"You believe in destiny?" Delangelo said. "Do you believe, with Dante, that God plants the soul individually in a man or woman, for a specific end, and that we therefore must follow our destiny without choice?"

"Well now, that's pretty complicated. If you're speaking of morality, what difference whether our destiny is predetermined or not, so long as we have the illusion of free choice? The illusion is our reality. As for the other part, about belief—no, I don't believe in God."

"Then how's your Dante coming along?"

Whiteside laughed. "I do believe in poetry. I can write about the *Commedia* without believing in God. In fact, I'm not so sure that Dante believed."

"This is fascinating," Delangelo said. "I'm sorry we didn't get together for lunch back in November. I would've liked talking with you about this."

"It was my fault. I got busy. I completely forgot. But what about this week? Tomorrow?"

"No, I have to go into the hospital tomorrow. I won't be fit for much for a month. It's radiation therapy." He gave a weak smile and said, "God gave me leukemia."

"Oh, I'm sorry. That's awful. But don't lose hope. Science does wonders these days. They can hold it in check, maybe cure it totally."

"'*Lasciate ogni speranza, voi ch'entrate*'—abandon all hope, you who enter."

"Dante put that over the gate to hell, not the door to the hospital. There's hope."

"Faith, hope, and love—these three," Delangelo said. "Your friend Bohm, there, seems to have faith. There's an implicate order, hidden within and under the explicate order where we live. From time to time, one of us, usually a scientist or a poet, catches a glimpse of that hidden order. The implicate order, a secret flower perpetually unfolding, but we're too blind, too set in our habits to see it. It's our nature to be blind—our fate. But the flower will unfold, the river become a sea, the linear become spherical, and the order be revealed, pretty much as in Dante."

"I see I'd better read this."

"You won't understand it all, unless you're a quantum physicist. But at least that's what he gets at generally, directly or by implication. He has faith, and therefore hope. I don't know about love. I'm a bit tired now. Would you mind?"

"Of course not. I didn't mean to stay. Here, what's the price on the book?"

Delangelo waved him off. "It's free. It's a gift. If you're destined to read it, how could I charge?"

"Would you like a visitor in the hospital?"

"Good Lord, no. I'll see you in about a month."

"Be well," Whiteside said. "I wish you luck."

"Luck, of one kind or another, was planted with me in the womb. But thank you."

Whiteside left.

* * *

She interrupted him. "Excuse me," she said, "but here we are, having dinner together. My name is Lena, yours is Filippo. Is that all right with you?"

"Lena," he said. "That means energy, vigor, nerve."

"It's short for Maddalena. As for vigor, who knows? I'm strong enough, I've had to be strong. My life hasn't been easy. Too many men. Men are beasts."

"Not all men," he said.

She laughed. "No, that's true. There are the Americans."

She was wearing a shawl-collared dress, electric blue, with a shiny finish to the cloth. The color made her eyes bright. She had served *crostini* as an appetizer, then an egg soup, and then roast chicken and a green salad. There had been plenty of wine.

"Americans," she said, "are romantics. They adore women. They put them up there, on the top of the mountain, and throw gifts up to them."

"Not all Americans," he said.

"True again. Some Americans are celibate." She gave him a heavy-lidded smile. "Either by inclination or necessity. Eh, Filippo?"

It was her hair that he recognized—thick, loosely curled, and metallic, with golden highlights. "I had a dream about you," he said. "Or at least you were in it. You were a contessa—you lived in a villa in Fiesole."

"Was it an exciting dream? What did we do?"

"It wasn't that kind of dream. You were married."

"To a beast, no doubt. Did I have a bruised face, a broken arm? Did I have a knife in my hand?"

"Heavens no. Not in my dream."

"In mine, then," she said. She thought for a moment, then said, "Haven't you been curious about me?"

"Your private life is none of my business. We all have private lives. You know nothing about mine, so why should I be curious about yours?"

"What an American! How fastidious and proper you are! Now, tell me the truth—haven't you wondered about me?"

"All right, yes, I've wondered a little. I can't understand how someone could, well, have so many visitors. And then there's what Signor Pulci said on the stairs that day."

"Signor Fleas. That's what *pulci* are. It's the right name for him. He sucks blood."

"So what *did* happen to your husband?"

"He died. He died when I put a kitchen knife between his ribs. Real life shocks you, eh? It was like killing an animal. He had broken my nose, he broke my jaw once, and he broke my arm. For myself, I could have endured it, but not for my daughter." She lifted her hands and let them drop. She looked around the dining room at the buffet, with a bouquet of chrysanthemums in a vase, at the china cupboard, at the glass-fronted display case of crystal glasses and decanters.

She said, "It would have been more fitting if I'd asked you for yesterday. You're a stranger in Florence, alone at Christmas. Why not bring cheer to a stranger's heart? I'll tell you why. It's because I always spend holidays with my daughter. She is twenty-three years old now, in a home for the helpless. You see, the treatment he gave me, he also gave to my daughter, when she was twelve. With his fist, he ruined her mind. She's a baby now. Yes, I have visitors. It costs to keep Genia where she is, and I too must eat."

Whiteside swallowed. "I'm sorry," he said. "You know, this is the second tragic story I've heard today. An acquaintance of mine just found out he has leukemia."

"I wish him luck. The world is full of tragic stories. I wish good luck to all of us." She got up and went to the buffet. She poured two pony glasses of cognac, brought one to him, and stood beside his chair. "To good luck," she said.

He had to stand up. They touched glasses, then drank. She said, "Is it that you don't like women?"

"I like women," he said. "But once burnt, twice shy."

She said, "A truly American proverb. In Italy it would be once burnt, then twice, then a thousand times, until nothing remains but ashes."

She refilled their glasses, brought the bottle to the table, and sat down again across from him. "Tell me how you got toasted," she said. "She must have been red hot."

"She was my wife," he said, "and everyone else's lover, as it turned out."

"Too much love, and not enough fidelity. Do you know something, Filippo? When you talk, you barely move your face. You keep your hands as still as a cat. Are you frozen? Why don't you open up, relax—and take off that tie! This is not a formal occasion. In fact, if you were to take off all your clothes, who would be the wiser?"

"To say she wasn't faithful would be the understatement of the year. Her name was Angie, for Angela—but she was no angel."

"Filippo, Signor Fiancobianco, Professor Whiteflank—pay attention to me."

"I am paying attention. Don't think I'm not. I'm sorry, Lena—it's nothing personal. Forgive me, but I just don't want to."

* * *

He read David Bohm's book and agreed with Delangelo that the implicate order was a given, an assumption, an unproved, unprovable axiom. He found it strange that a physicist should think so much like a platonist and that a book so filled with the language of quantum theory should be, at bottom, so nearly analogous to Dante's great idea. He recalled reading that Plato, in all his writings, equated God and Ideal Form only three times. But Plotinus had made God the name of the Ideal, and the Fathers of the Church had completed the transformation. The spirit wanted to move upward toward God, but flesh was heavy. So God helped. His grace and mercy were everywhere in the phenomenal world. In Dante, God enclosed the universe, moved it with His love, sent light and love into it. To Dante the pilgrim, He sent Beatrice as a guide through the heavenly spheres. She brought him to the great symbolic yellow rose, the heavenly counterpart of earth's red rose of desire.

Whiteside remembered an article he'd read, "Out of Plato's Cave," by J. T. Fraser, which dealt with man's participation in time. Fraser contended that Plato's true heirs were the modern scientists who worked on the assumption that order existed and that its principles were there to be discovered. So perhaps it wasn't so strange, after all, that a physicist should speak like a poet, though without any attribution to a Creator.

Eager to talk, Whiteside haunted the bookstore all through January. But Delangelo was never there. His assistant, a woman of about forty, sat at his desk and consistently gave Whiteside the same news, a fatalistic shrug.

But in mid-February, again on a Sunday morning, Whiteside glanced in at the window and saw him. He reached out to tap the glass, but stopped. Delangelo looked terrible. He had lost most of his hair, and the bones of his skull and face stood out. He had the glazed look of someone who'd been tortured. Whiteside withdrew his hand and went on by.

Within a month after that, he had finished his essay, revised it, and was satisfied. It wasn't a scholarly piece of work in the usual sense; it was rather like a reading of, a loving commentary upon, a magnificent poem, by a scholar who knew it intimately. It was good work, inspired work. In writing of Dante's River of Light, which contained all the bright fragments of partial existence, as it suddenly expanded and became the Sea of Wholeness, Whiteside's passion rose as Dante's had risen, and he expressed himself in prose as precise and controlled as Dante's verse.

Finally, near the end of March, he found Delangelo in his shop, looking much improved. It was a Wednesday, the aisles were crowded, but Whiteside rushed to the desk and said, "Welcome back, old friend. I have finished my essay. Would you read it? I have a hundred things to talk to you about. Could we have lunch? Today?"

Delangelo held up a hand. "I'm weak. I must hoard my strength. But perhaps this Friday?"

"Wonderful. You know, coming to Florence was the best thing I ever did. It's like stepping into another dimension. My mind never felt so wide awake, so alive."

Delangelo made an effort to smile. It looked as if his gums had receded. "My mind slowed down," he said. "I entered another dimension, too. I took two steps toward the East. In the East, what's a mind? What's an intellect? I'm not sure I could understand your essay anymore."

"But will you read it?"

"Bring it on Friday. I'll try."

Whiteside hesitated, then said, "I don't know you, and you don't know me, but I've really been looking forward to seeing you."

"Did you pray for me? Someone must have, for here I am. Until Friday, then."

* * *

How fine to have finished a work! What exhilaration! To wake up in the morning and say, "Now what shall we do?"—it was nothing short of bliss. Now he truly felt that he was on sabbatical. He had put in a hard six days, and had earned a day of rest and pleasure. Too busy until now to explore Florence, he would remedy that lack, and why not spend a few weeks in Rome and Naples, say the month of May? Of course, he mustn't forget Ravenna and Dante's tomb. He owed a pilgrimage there.

On Friday he didn't find Delangelo at the bookstore. His assistant said, "Signor Delangelo is very ill. He has sent for his daughter in New York." Whiteside extended the manuscript, but took it back. If the man was so ill as to send for his daughter, he was too ill to read. "Please give him my best wishes," he said.

Easter was cold and rainy. Whiteside had asked Lena to dinner, in the evening, after her visit to her daughter. When he stopped by for her, she put on a dark brown fur coat. "Is that mink?" he said. She said, "Yes, I think so. Do you like it?"

"It's beautiful."

"I don't embarrass you, then?"

"Of course not. Why . . . ?" But then he saw. "No, you don't embarrass me," he said.

He took her to the White Boar, an *osteria* on the other side of the Arno. The conversation didn't go well. She seemed preoccupied. "You're thinking of your daughter," he said.

"Yes, and other things. I have to change my life, Filippo. I'm forty-five years old. A man of forty-five is in his prime, but a woman is done for, *finita.*"

"I wouldn't say that. There must be things you can do. Get a job somewhere, start a business."

"A business requires money. As for a job, I'm a criminal, don't forget. It's a matter of record. Who would hire me?"

A depression settled in. They finished dinner and walked back over the bridge. She said, "Do you like music? A week from Saturday, there's a concert at Santa Trinita. Would you go with me?"

"I would, yes. Thank you."

He let them into the lobby. She said, "Don't you look into your mailbox? That letter came on Friday."

He opened the box. They walked upstairs. "I hate this stairway," she said. "I hate this cold weather."

"At least you have a nice warm coat."

"It's not new. A friend got it for me. It used to belong to a contessa, maybe the one in your dream." On the landing, she said, "Would you like to come in for a drink?"

He saw that her heart wasn't in it. "Thank you, but not tonight."

She glanced at the letter. "A girlfriend, eh? A young one—a student."

"Good night," he said.

In his bedroom, he read the letter, and then remembered: the girl he'd met at the consulate. Her name was Ellen Fairfax. She lived in Detroit. His advice had worked, her friend was safe in California, and she planned to come to Florence in May, perhaps to stay for a while. She planned to call on him and thank him in person.

He couldn't remember what advice he'd given.

* * *

He'd had dinner, with half a liter of wine, at the *rosticceria* in Via della Spada. He had walked along the Arno afterward, and had stopped for a brandy at a bar. He wasn't drunk. He felt pleasantly disengaged. His good feeling took him lightly up the stairs, where he unlocked both locks, breathed for a few seconds, then touched the light switch.

Hell, the power was off. It wasn't the first time. He'd bought some candles for such emergencies. If it wasn't the power, it was the water. In winter, when the river was high, the current swept layers of plastic bags off the bottom and clogged the screened intake for the city's water supply. He'd gone as long as a week without a shower. He kept a reserve supply of bottled water for making coffee and emergency shaving.

He went upstairs, hung his raincoat on the peg outside the bedroom, then continued on up to find the candles. By the dim light filtering through the cracks in the shutters, he saw the open window, the broken glass. He whirled and got his arm up in time to take the first blow on his left wrist. He kicked out at a shape, heard a grunt, and then swung his fist. He hit someone, all right, but lightning flashed in his eyes. He was on the floor, curled to protect himself against the kicks. There were two men, he thought. They were trying to kill him. They worked in silence. That noise was coming from his own throat.

* * *

He drifted toward, away from, death. The boat moved over black water. Faces appeared, then vanished. There were nurses, nuns, a doctor. Lena's face was so grief-stricken that he wondered if her daughter had died. He couldn't speak, his jaws were wired shut, and the blows had done something to his ears. Mouths moved, speaking to him, but all he could hear was a high whine like some transmission from outer space. He would have told

Lena something to comfort her, but even if he could have found the words, he couldn't have spoken them.

At one point came a clown of some sort, wearing a wrinkled, ravaged-looking red mask. The eyes were tiny and desperate, and there was a hand that wouldn't let go of his own. Or maybe it wasn't a mask, for tears were rolling down the scored cheeks, and the mouth worked, twisted, jerked up and down. Whiteside tried to say, "Get away from me. Who are you? I can't hear you." But only a bubbling sound escaped around the wires. Then the man was on his knees beside the bed, gripping, kissing Whiteside's hand. Then he was gone. The nightmare ended.

Gradually, he learned to separate day and night. He began to hurt more. But his hearing began coming back. He made a writing motion and a nun brought him a notepad and pen. He managed to write "Knee, Arm, Jaw, Eye, Ears. What else?" The nun took the note and scurried away.

That evening a doctor stood by his bed. "Can you hear me?" Whiteside nodded. "Good. The blows shocked your auditory nerves, but they're repairing themselves. You have been badly hurt."

Whiteside pointed to the bandage covering his right eye. The doctor said, "No, the eye is fine. You have a cut in the eyebrow— 12 stitches. On your head, 138 stitches. Three ribs broken, wrist broken, knee broken. The knee was *gratuito,* free. Someone had to arrange you, prop you deliberately, to break it that way. Lucky for you it wasn't both knees. You'll be here for six weeks, eating soup."

Lena visited again, and this time the scene was real. "Who found me?"

"I did. I heard a thump at my door, I looked, and there was your blood. I called the police and the ambulance. You were naked. The villains had left you at my door."

The word *mascalzoni,* villains, struck Whiteside as funny. Was this a stage comedy, then, with heroes and villains? Lena said, "Why are you laughing?"

"I'm trying not to—it hurts. What about the things in my apartment, my manuscripts?"

"Don't worry about that. You're alive. Worry about getting well."

"Tell the people here that I have insurance. The company will pay them."

She laughed. "They know. Would they have repaired you without hope of payment? You haven't learned the first thing about Florence."

"How did they find out?"

"In matters of money, your consul is most helpful."

* * *

Before the middle of May, before he was really ready, he wanted out. The doctor advised him to stay. But his ribs had knit, his head was healing, and he'd been practicing with the crutches in the hallway. The doctor shrugged. "It's your choice." Though shorter than Whiteside, and wider, he brought in a roll of clothing as a gift. To accommodate the cast, he cut off one leg of the trousers; the other leg came down to midway on Whiteside's calf. He slit the jacket sleeve to the elbow; it flapped around the arm cast. There was underwear, a sock, a sweater. On his good foot, he wore the hospital slipper. When he was dressed, the doctor said seriously, "I think we should have let you die."

He had a point. The mirror gave back a head still bristly from being shaved, deeply scarred on top and along both sides, and a right eye that drooped in a lewd, perpetual wink. He had lost weight. His neck was as scrawny as a turkey's, and loose folds of skin hung below his jaw. The sturdiest feature in the face, the mouth, was dependable only because the wires held it in place.

The doctor signed the release. Whiteside signed the blue claim form for his insurance company. He took the elevator down and crutched his way to the street. It was a long two blocks to his house. He had to think about, order, and arrange the disparate particulars of every step he took.

He didn't have a key to the building anymore. He rang Lena's bell. Her voice came from the speaker: *Chi è?*"

"Filippo."

"Senta, aspetti là. Vengo."

He didn't wait. When she unlocked the door, he went inside and was halfway up the first flight before she came down. "Filippo, you can't," she said.

"I will, by God. Help me. Give me a hand here."

He never could have made it without her. She took his left crutch away and replaced it with herself. With his arm over her shoulder, hers around his waist, they progressed up the stairs, one step at a time.

On the top landing, he said, "We might as well go on up. I want to salvage what I can from up there."

"You don't have the keys," she said. "Anyway, there's nothing to salvage. The rooms have been cleaned, repairs made. In fact, the apartment has been rented to someone else."

"Hey, wait, now—I paid the rent through August."

She opened her door. "Let's get you inside. You look awful, like they buried you by mistake and you escaped. Those clothes!"

He hadn't seen this part of her apartment. There were two bedrooms. They went past the more elaborate one. In the smaller, plain room, she said, "This is my bed, do you understand? Here, let me help you undress."

He resisted. "I have things to do. I need a new passport, I have to replace my traveler's checks. God almighty, I have to start all over here. I have no money, nothing."

"You have some new clothes—look." She opened a closet and showed him a gray wool suit with one long leg, one cut off. On the coat, one sleeve had been hemmed just below the elbow, to accommodate his wrist cast. "See, here's a briefcase to carry things in, and here's a toilet kit for your razor and toothbrush. I saved those things. Everything else was destroyed or stolen. What wreckage!"

Talking as she worked, she helped him out of his jacket and sweater. "I made a deal with Luigi. In return for certain considerations, he would retrieve your rent money, subtract a small fee, and—how on earth did you get into those pants? By the way, someone called for you. It was a man and, I think, a woman. I told them you had returned to America, that your apartment had already been rented."

"Luigi?"

"*Sì*, Signor Pulci. Stop that! Don't you want to try on your new silk underwear?"

"Luigi Pulci was a fifteenth-century poet. His patron was Lorenzo de' Medici. He was a madman. He wrote a combination epic poem and farce, called *Morgante Maggiore.*"

"How do you remember things like that?" she said. "Anyway, this Luigi is a cheat and a miser. I'm not even sure he can write. There now, lie back. I'll lift the leg up." She observed him from head to toe. "Well, at least that didn't get broken," she said. "That's a major consolation."

She closed the drape, switched on the small bedside lamp, stepped from her slippers, and dropped her blue robe. He said, "Lena?"

"Signor Fiancobianco, shut up. There aren't many things I can do in this world, but those that I can do, I do to perfection.

* * *

He stayed until the middle of June. His hair grew out over his scars, but the lascivious droop of his right eye seemed permanent. He had to learn to talk without all that metal in his mouth. Permanent as well was the rigidity of his knee, which refused to bend once the cast was removed. The doctor suggested a course of physical therapy. "Better yet," he said, "have a plastic joint installed. American doctors are geniuses. They can replace any part of the human body. *Ecco,* you're a new man."

Without his casts but still on crutches, Whiteside hobbled to the bookstore in Piazza Carlo Goldoni. There was a new sign over the door: IL BIBLIOFILO. But he recognized Delangelo's assistant at the desk. He asked. She shrugged and said, *"È morto."*

At the train station, Lena saw him onto the express for Rome. From Rome he would fly to San Francisco by way of New York. From San Francisco it was a one-hour flight to Arcata, where the chairman of his department would meet him. He would stay at a motel until his house was vacated, and then, his adventure over, he would plunge into the quotidian again.

Lena wore her electric blue dress to the station. She carried his briefcase and his new suitcase. At the train, she said, "Climb up, find a seat, and I'll hand your bags in through the window."

It was all he could do to mount the two high steps. Noticing his frustration, Lena pushed him from behind. He got a seat by the window, though, and as Lena lifted the bags he caught them and stowed them in the overhead rack. From the platform, she said, "I love you with my soul as well, Filippo. Please come back. Will you?"

"I promise," he said. "Until then, I will hold you in my heart."

She laughed. "Ah," she said, "you have become Italian. You're hopeless."

Hopeless? A physical wreck, yes, and without a page of manuscript to show for his year's work, but without hope?

The train moved. He leaned out. She trotted a few steps, then stopped. The wheels clicked on the switches, faster and faster. The last he saw of her was the brilliant, diminishing blue of her dress.

Memory

"Mike? Mike Martin? Is that you?" The voice came from behind him. American, Midwestern, shrill in calling. He turned. "Ellen, what a surprise."

"I had no idea you were still in Florence," she said. "Imagine running into you like this, just when I need you. It makes me believe in destiny. What are you doing? I mean, right now?"

"I was going to lunch," he said.

"Come on, then—it's just down this street, Via what's its name. You can't imagine the trouble I've been having."

"What sort of trouble?"

"There is this man—a professor? I met him last November at the American Consulate. God, I was crazy with worry, and they wouldn't do anything for me. It was the bitter end, believe me. Anyway, this nice professor stopped and helped me out. He really made sense. I want to thank him. It's the least I can do, don't you think?"

"Sounds reasonable," he said. "What's his name?"

She stopped at a tall door. "Here it is. Whiteside. I rang some doorbells, but all I got was garble. Professor Whiteside."

"Let's try Luzzi," he said. He pressed a bell button. The speaker crackled, then a woman said, *"Chi è là?"* Michael asked for Professor Whiteside. The woman said that the professor had returned to America. When Michael Englished the news, Ellen said, "Is the apartment for rent?" Michael asked. The woman said, *"È occupato già,"* and the speaker clicked off.

"It's already rented," he said. "So you're planning to stay in Florence?"

"I've dreamed of it since, well, since you left to come here. I love this city. It's my favorite in all of Europe. I didn't get to see it in November, because of the disaster. But now I'm free. I want to learn it, really get to know it. God, isn't it beautiful?"

The way she talked made him flinch. That bubbling, American optimism came from having life too easy, from not knowing enough. He avoided Americans in Florence. He wouldn't want this one living within striking distance. "It's beautiful because it's May," he said. "In another month, it'll be summer, hot as a furnace. Mosquitoes, too. If you think Vermont mosquitoes are vicious, try these."

"Pooh, Mike. If you can stand it, I can. You've lived here, what, eight years?" She took him by the arm. She was as tall as he, angular, Anglo-Saxon, from Detroit. They had met at Middlebury College. She'd been a poet, trying, with some other student writers, to start a new literary magazine. He had done the cover for the first issue: a bunch of cherry blossoms and a lone feather, so sharply drawn that the figures jumped from the surface. Magic realism. Dead and buried.

"Do you still write poems?"

"God no, Mike. I had no talent, face it. It was all romantic yearning, a protracted adolescence. I work for an insurance company back home in Detroit, or I did. I quit my job—I'm free now." She held his arm and sort of bounced along beside him. That was another thing about American women: they tried to remain girls, perpetually athletic. This one made him think of peppermint.

"It's a miracle, finding you," she breathed. "Let me take you to lunch. I've got money. Tell me what you've been up to. You can begin teaching me about Florence, you old expatriate. What street is this?"

"It translates as the Street of the Sword. It runs into the Street of the Sun and the Street of Beautiful Women. Where are you staying?"

"At the Hotel Baglioni, till I find a place. But you, you must have a neat apartment by now, with a studio, I'll bet. Are you painting?"

"Actually, no. I work at the Institute for Art Restoration. I live in Fiesole, up in the hills to the north. I ride the bus to work. But here, this is the Antinori Palace. *Buca* means hole. We'll have lunch in the *buca* under the palace."

They went downstairs into a large, vaulted cellar whose walls were papered with posters from the world over. The headwaiter led them to a table in a corner. She said, "How totally romantic." She opened the menu and said, "I love Italian food—I want some of everything."

"Seafood antipasto?" he said. "Tagliatelle with carbonara sauce? Lombatina? That's a veal chop."

"Sounds wonderful," she said. "And don't forget the wine. I love wine."

Their waiter, a gray-haired man in black trousers and a white shirt, set a basket of bread on the table. Michael ordered. He asked for a bottle of Antinori Chianti and a large mineral water.

"You speak beautifully," she said. "You've really become Italian. You don't even look American anymore. Your clothes, your manner. You're a real foreigner."

"Americans seem foreign to me. English is such a strange, unpleasant language—it never escapes fully from the mouth. Half the thoughts and feelings stay inside. Italians are much more open."

As if playing the demonstrative Italian, their waiter flourished two plates of antipasto, set them on the table, and said, *"Ecco! Buon appetito!"* There were squid, small clams, mussels, and crayfish, arranged around cold parsleyed potatoes. Michael said, "Try a little oil on the potatoes."

Then the wine and water were borne in. The waiter opened the bottles, poured a little wine into Michael's glass, and held his breath. Michael tasted. *"È buono,"* he said, and the waiter, in ecstasy, filled their glasses.

Michael raised his glass. *"Salute—*your health."

"Whoa, wait," she said. "To destiny, fate, accident. To the good luck that brought our paths together today. To miracles." She touched her glass to his.

Her face was too long, her nose not quite straight. She wore her brown hair short and uncurled. Except for her eyes, she was plain, and her eyes could have been more striking, more green and mysterious, if she'd learned the art of shading. A master would have enlarged those eyes, set them a bit farther apart and deepened them, to make the face focus just there, to lessen its length. But she hadn't been made by a master. She'd been made by Mr. and Mrs. Fairfax in Detroit.

"Umm, delicious," she said. "And this wine, my God! I'm surprised that Italians aren't drunk all the time." She drank the glass straight down. He refilled it. She said, "Do you believe in destiny, in miracles? I do. Otherwise, how do you explain our having lunch together in this what do you call it?"

"Buca," he said.

"Anyway, it's strange, isn't it? It's nice, but strange."

"Miracles I don't know about," he said. "But destiny, yes. I was conceived to do just what I'm doing. From birth I set out on the road. And here I am."

"Having lunch with me."

"That, too," he said. "But what I meant was . . ."

The waiter removed their plates and set down wide bowls of pasta in egg sauce. He gave them a bowl of grated cheese and filled their glasses with the wine. Michael said, "Deep inside, I've always known I was somebody else."

"Somebody else? Jesus, that's weird. Who?"

The waiter passed on the way to another table, and Ellen flashed him a brilliant smile. For an instant, she was beautiful. He caught his breath. She didn't look American or Italian.

The moment fled and she was saying, "Like an alter ego?"

"Not another personality, if that's what you mean." He hesitated. "A few years ago, my mother had our genealogy done. Like everyone's, our family tree is a mixture—German, Irish, and French, of course. The name Martin goes back to a French Huguenot who lived in Lyon. In 1570 he married Isabella Martini, who came from Florence. A Martin and a Martini, think of it."

"My friend Sylvie's mother came from Florence," she said. "What a coincidence. You could be related to Sylvie. I hope the same thing doesn't happen to you that happened to her."

"Ellen, listen to me. It explains why I learned Italian so easily, why I'm so good at my work. Not many Americans make it as art restorers in Florence. Florence is world-famous for art restoration. But I've made it here because, well, I somehow know things I couldn't possibly know. Say a painting is to be restored—a painting done before Michelangelo's death in 1564. Well, I can look at it and tell what it was like when it was new. It's as if I have a photo of it in my head. I can see it."

"It's not that I don't believe you, Mike. But say you do have pictures in your head. How do you know they're accurate?"

"When I came here, I didn't know a word of Italian, but within a year I was fluent. It was strange—I would look at a sentence and suddenly know what it meant. The Tuscan dialect has certain peculiarities in structure and pronunciation. I seemed to know them already. Studying Italian was like archaeology for me—I took off a few layers and there it was. I could read Dante the first time I tried."

"Try that with German. German's a bitch. Do you suppose we could have a little more wine?"

He called the waiter over and said, *"Un'altra."* He pointed to the bottle. To Ellen he said, "One day at the institute, they were discussing how to remove a fresco from the old refectory in All Saints' Church. I said, 'Where is it?' They told me and I said, 'Be careful, there's a Bondone under it. The Virgin and Child, with John the Baptist.' I knew it was there, and sure enough they found traces of a fresco, close enough to Giotto's style that they could attribute it."

"Bondone is Giotto?" Her eyes wandered, then brightened as the waiter approached. When he filled her glass, she said, "Thank you," and gave off that smile again.

Michael refused the wine, took a glass of mineral water, and said, "Giotto was Dante's contemporary, late thirteenth and early fourteenth century."

"Do you mind?" she said. She broke a piece of bread and wiped her bowl clean. "This is so good," she said. With food in her mouth, she said, "You really get into your work, don't you? But you're talking reincarnation, not alter egos. I believe in reincarnation. I think we all come back sometime. It stands to reason."

"You don't believe I just remember?"

"Well, frankly," she said. "Look, you and I were born in 1953. It would be really rare if . . . Not that I think you're lying or anything."

The waiter picked up her pasta bowl. To Martin he said, *"Ha finito, signore?"*

"Yes, I've finished."

The chops came on platters, with roasted potatoes, and the salads were huge. Martin said, "In Florence, to eat well means to eat much."

"But you're thin as a stick."

"I eat once a day, and I walk a lot."

"Where do you eat?" she said. "In Fiesole?"

"Yes. I have rooms in a villa."

"Like an apartment house?"

"A private home. A contessa owns it. I eat what her cook prepares. It's a good arrangement for me."

"I'll bet it is," she said.

"She's nearly sixty."

"I meant it's good you get to eat once in a while, that's all." She busied herself with the veal, but she was slowing down now. Michael had stopped eating. He watched her jaws move as she chewed. Her eyes glazed over and her mouth worked.

He cleared his throat. "For dessert, we can go heavy or light. How do you feel?"

"I can't eat another bite, Mike. I weigh a ton."

"In that case, espresso and brandy." He caught the waiter's attention.

He felt as if he'd crossed a shaky bridge. But now he was past it and the rest was anticlimax. When the brandy and coffee came, he said, "Tell me about your Professor Whiteside."

She rolled her head slightly, and her eyes focused on him. "He's not mine. I only barely met him." Her speech slurred a little. She said, "We were on this tour—twenty cities in a month? The tour leader was a big German woman, with a German mentality. She didn't like us—I mean Sylvie and me—because we were always going off on our own. Anyway, at Pisa we lost Sylvie. She just vanished. We were waiting for the train, she went back to the station for something, and poof! It was on the way from Paris to Rome, with a day in Florence. This fat German said get on the train, I said not without Sylvie, and she said if you leave the tour I'm not responsible, shit!"

Her face was lopsided. It kept losing its shape. She lifted a hand and dropped it. "I said good-bye to the tour. I thought I could catch up in Rome, or maybe Athens, but no such luck. Did you ever try to get through to the carabinieri? Talk about a German mentality. When they found her, I couldn't get a word out of them, and the doctors were worse. There she was with tubes in her nose and wires connecting her to a machine—intensive care, you know?—and those idiots kept saying there was nothing wrong with her. She had black eyes, she didn't even recognize me. Her passport was gone. Some fisherman had found her on the beach. That's when I got on the train for Florence."

He watched her. He said, "That's where you met the professor."

She laughed bitterly. "At the American Consulate, they hate Americans. An American gets nothing there—they won't move. They would make inquiries, they said. They gave me an appointment with the consul in a week—a week! I was a wreck. I sat in the lobby, tearing my hair, crying, having fits. Then this man knelt down and said what's wrong. I blurted out the whole sad story. He asked if I knew anyone important back home. I didn't, but my dad did, an old friend, a senator from Ohio. The professor said you call your dad and tell him to call the senator. Which is what happened. The senator jumped on the State Department, they jumped on the ambassador in Rome, and he jumped all over the consul here. They got Sylvie's mother to come to Pisa and take her home."

He waited, but she seemed to be finished. She looked over at him, her head tilted slightly, her eyes large and luminous. He said, "Well? What happened to Sylvie?"

"Oh," she said. "I don't really know. I hadn't met her before the tour. When I got home, I called. We write letters back and forth. In fact, I went to see her in California, to persuade her to come on this trip with me, but she wouldn't. Her family lives in the Napa Valley, near San Francisco. Her dad's a wine maker. They're Italian. It's a tight family. I asked her what happened, but she wouldn't say."

"Her parents must have been grateful for what you did. You really stuck by her."

"Oh, they were—they're nice. They come from around here, or at least her mother does. And Sylvie and I are friends. She's not the kind to forget."

"Would you like more coffee?"

"You must be shocked, Mike. I'm ashamed of myself, running off at the mouth. Getting drunk. I drink too much, I know . . ."

"Forget it—it could happen to anyone."

"It's nice of you to say so. You're kind, Mike, you really are."

He called for the check, then laid out the money to cover it.

"I invited you," she said. "Let me pay."

"It's paid—my pleasure," he said.

"Well, next time, then. I'll be sober, I promise."

"Listen," he said. He made sure her eyes were on him, then said, "In the year 1310, Michele Martini, the older brother of the Sienese painter Simone Martini, was living in Via dell'Inferno, not far from here. It was a dark, narrow, rat-infested street, a caldron in summer and a river of ice in winter. Michele's younger brother had the Holy Spirit in his fingers, he was already famous beyond Siena, he was the town's authentic genius. With a brother like that, what was Michele to do? Are you listening?"

Her eyelids were drooping. He snapped his fingers and she lifted her head. "This Michele," he said, "had no defined talents such as his brother had. He spoke well, in a voice soft yet round—precise, clear, and persuasive. He had a fine eye for colors, textures, and shapes. He could distinguish among the hundred shades of blue so unerringly that his brother, who lived with color, was astonished. He knew more about machines than anyone else in Florence. But he was not an artist.

"Do you know what it means to have exceptional abilities, but no art? It is hell on earth, believe me. Michele's brother's gifts, though fewer, were concentrated all in the same direction, and each of his paintings was more stunning than the last. As if God guided him, he gave his vision to the world, while Michele labored in one workshop after another, a functionary earning his daily bread and little more. He lived with a widow on the top floor of the tallest house in Hell Street.

"In 1312, at age thirty, he fell in love with a beautiful girl named Alessandra. After fierce battles, the widow permitted him to bring the girl into the house. They were married and had children. Their children had children. In 1343 he died, a year before his famous brother died. Alessandra lived on for many years. As I see it, I have fifteen years to go."

With an effort, she lifted her head. "What? What's her name, the contessa?"

"It's not important," he said. "Let's go, shall we? We both could use some air."

They went upstairs and out into the street.

"You live on the top floor?" she said. "It must be nice. Could I see your place sometime?"

"I don't know, maybe. We'll see."

She took his hand and leaned heavily on him. He steered her toward the Baglioni. For a moment, when she flashed that smile, he had thought she might be the one. But now he looked at all the women on the street, the female river flowing by.

The Violation

Anyone who knowingly walks into the wolf's mouth deserves to be eaten. But to what extent had Sylvia Passini known? Well, she was twenty-one years old, a graduate of Stanford, and a veteran of a few wars with men. Not exactly a lamb in the ways of the world. Then, too, she had felt the danger, and to feel is to know. So, she had known and been thrilled by it, thrilled to follow where that man took her, and the rest is history.

It began at the train station in Pisa, where a mixed group of Americans were standing on the platform, awaiting the train to Florence. The group had gathered in New York and given themselves over to their shepherd, Matthilde Weisskopf, who led by holding aloft her umbrella with a red scarf tied to the ferrule, but who was also capable of nipping from behind. Sylvie didn't care for the tour director, didn't like being driven in lockstep through city after city—but her parents had insisted. First with a tour, they said, and later alone, when you have more experience.

In New York she had met Ellen Fairfax, who worked for an insurance company in Detroit. Ellen was thirty years old, somewhat angular, and had a habit of walking with her arms crossed over her chest. If Sylvie didn't like Frau Weisskopf, Ellen hated her, hated the other Americans on the tour, and hated whatever city they happened to be in. Sylvie guessed that there was a reason for so much bitterness, but she didn't pry. Ellen's troubles were her own business; she would confide if she wanted to; if not, not. One good quality she had: she was willing to take a chance. She and Sylvie leaped the fence at every opportunity, pleased to make Frau Weisskopf show her fangs and growl.

On the platform in Pisa, Sylvie said, "Watch the bags, I'll get us something to munch on." She dashed across two sets of tracks, violating the DANGER—FORBIDDEN signs, and went to a vendor's stand in the station. Happening to glance up from the pears and apples, she saw a man leaning against a doorframe, watching her. His eyes were hard and insistent, his mouth a tight, unpleasant curl. He raised a hand, snapped his fingers, and beckoned her over.

Why did she go? No matter, she went. He took her arm loosely —she could have broken away at any time—and guided her outside to a van. She could have refused to get in, but didn't. Once in the van, of course, she couldn't go back and refuse.

There was another man in the van—his name was Ugo—and he was in charge of the lemonade. From the jump seat behind the driver, he smiled and offered a glass of lemonade, and she drank it. Did she suspect that there was something in it? How could she not have thought, Alcohol—drugs? But she drank it right down. It wasn't long before she was seeing things. The sea swelled up in a gigantic ball, exuding streams of plus and minus signs, and engulfed the land. A cliff, like the side of a great glazed cake, slid silently down into frothy water. It was so strange, this world, that she laughed and laughed.

The driver's name was Ruggiero. He and Ugo had no idea that she understood Italian, so they talked, and she understood not only what they said, but what they were going to say. To have such understanding was exhilarating, it gave her power over them and made her their master. See how close they stayed to her? That was because they hadn't the power to leave without permission. She wouldn't give permission. She toyed with them. She laughed secretly.

Ugo said, "Viareggio." She could see right through her clothes to her naked body. Her sight had never been so keen. She saw through Ruggiero's clothing, and Ugo's. They hated her for her power over them and tried to escape, but she wouldn't let them. They hit her and tried smothering her with their weight, but she breathed right through the floor of the van, drew air into her lungs between the wide-spaced molecules of steel. The hitting was nothing, it was like the loose slap of a table napkin in her face—it kept the mosquitoes away. The word for mosquitoes was *zanzare,* which sounded like mosquitoes. "Zzz," she said, and laughed.

Sometimes it was day and sometimes night. There was a Luigi, a Salvatore, a Domenico. There was a *spiaggia,* which her heart knew meant beach. Then there were only Ruggiero and Ugo, then Ugo alone. She lost her powers and even Ugo escaped. But the sand was warm. She put her ear to it and heard the sea humming in a deep bass voice.

A scavenger found her, an old man with a sack who made his living from the beach, and he called the police and they ordered an ambulance. She floated to a hospital in Pisa. They asked who she was, and she wouldn't tell them. Her identification was hidden deep inside, where even Ugo and his friends hadn't been able to find it. She still had the power to keep a secret.

She woke up, hurting inside and out, and glad enough to tell them her name. Just in time, she clamped her teeth shut. Only her name escaped. She remembered what a thing she'd done at the station. Had she really followed those leather pants into a van? She fell asleep again, then woke. In one of the intervals, she found Ellen Fairfax by her bed, talking to doctors and the police. She told Ellen her name, but not a word about Ruggiero, Ugo, and the others, for they would say she'd gone willingly, submitting to anything they wanted, even if they wanted to kill her.

"Oh, Sylvie, your hair." Sylvie squinted. If walls could bend, then her mother might not be her mother. "Sylvie, Sylvie," the woman said, in her mother's voice. She awakened again and said, "Mother?"

"Yes, I'm right here, I won't go away. You're safe now. Just sleep, I'll be right beside you." It was just as when she'd had pneumonia and almost died.

She slept, and then the tube was gone from her nose. Beside her bed was another bed, rumpled, and she saw that her mother had rented part of the hospital. Leave it to Mother—Mother could do anything. "How did you find me?"

"We got a call from the State Department in the middle of the night. Mario drove me to San Francisco and put me on the first flight to Rome. And here I am."

"Ellen, it must have been. Is she here? She was here—I think she was."

"They didn't mention an Ellen," her mother said. "There was a Senator somebody. He told them you'd been . . . hurt, and they called us right away."

"It was Ellen Fairfax, I'm sure. I shouldn't have done that to Ellen."

"Done what, honey?"

She couldn't answer. Her mother took her hand and squeezed hard. "The important thing is you're alive. That's all that matters. I love you so much, Sylvie." Then her mother was crying. She cried as if looking down into a casket. Sylvie thought what it would be like to have her mother looking down on her in that way, but if it was a casket, she wouldn't know, would she?

She closed her eyes and slept. When she woke up this time, there was real sunlight coming in at the real window. The nurse said, *"Eccola—buon giorno!"* Then her mother put some plastic bags on the other bed and spoke to the nurse rapidly in Italian.

The Violation

Sylvie didn't comprehend a word of it, but whatever it was, it made the nurse laugh. Her mother laughed, too, then turned to Sylvie. "It's time to get up. They're kicking you out. Hospitals are for sick people. I brought you some things—put them on. Let's go to Florence."

She'd been up before, to step to the bathroom, but this time the floor stayed where it was. She opened the sacks. In the bathroom, she stacked the clothing on the commode and removed her hospital gown.

There was her body. Strange body. She looked down at the hill her abdomen made, at her hipbones, at the yellowish bruises on her thighs. Were those the same breasts? The contours seemed different. The fist marks were certainly different. She stooped to the commode and quickly covered herself with the high-waisted cotton underpants, the plain cotton bra. She pulled on the nylons and quickly dropped the slip over her head. Then came the skirt, blouse, sweater, and shoes. When nothing but her hands and face were showing, she looked for the first time at the mirror.

They'd hacked her hair off with the knife, leaving crude patches. Green bruises spread out under her eyes, and her left eyebrow had been shaved, and a cut stitched. With the hair gone, her neck seemed long, and she found a bruise beneath her right ear.

When she went out, her mother said, "Oh dear, let me fix that." From her purse, she took a long white scarf. She wound it around Sylvie's head and pinned it with a brooch. Sylvie said, "Thank you." She knew why her mother had held back the scarf and pin: it was so Sylvie wouldn't have to face the mirror if she didn't want to.

"You look like the Queen of Sheba," her mother said. "How do you feel? Are you ready?"

Sylvie shook the nurse's hand. "Thank you—good-bye." The nurse said, *"Addio, signorina, signora."* Sylvie's mother said, *"Grazie per la vostra gentilezza."*

The nurse insisted on carrying the suitcase as far as the street door, where there were more good-byes. Sylvie reached to take it then, but her mother brushed her away. A man got out of a car parked at the curb. He carried the bag, and when he'd opened the rear door for them, he put the bag in the trunk. He then drove not to the station, but out of town, heading east.

"Mother," Sylvie said. "We could've taken the train."

"No more trains for a while. And don't forget, in Italy I'm rich."

The money came from an inheritance. Her mother's parents had left her a large farm near Greve, not far from Florence, and she'd sold it a long time ago, before Sylvie was born. By Italian law, the money couldn't be taken out of the country, so the Passinis came over every few years for a free vacation. On their last trip, when Sylvie was still in high school, they'd gone to see the farm, a mustard-colored stone house, with barns and shops and sheds, standing amid rolling vineyards and olive groves. It was a little like their own place in the Napa Valley, though, of course, Mario grew only grapes.

"Are you going to buy a car this time?" They always bought a car when they came to Italy.

"I don't know—would you like one? The first priority is getting you some clothes. You'll need a suitcase, a handbag, toilet things. We'll start from scratch, what do you say? Florence is a wonderful place to shop."

From scratch, yes. She'd left the hospital with nothing but what she had on. "I could use some shoes," she said. "These are too small."

"I had to guess at the size. We'll throw them out."

"Mother, listen, you don't have to spend a lot of money on me —I'm fine, really. You didn't have to rent a car just to avoid the train station. A train station won't throw me into shock. You shouldn't waste your money."

"What I spend on you won't be wasted," her mother said, and squeezed her hand.

In Florence the driver took them to the Hotel Minerva, on Piazza Santa Maria Novella. It was where they always stayed. This time she had booked a suite of rooms, on the third floor front, where they had a view of the odd-shaped piazza with its two marble obelisks, the facade of the cathedral, the shops and restaurants, pigeons, people, and the Loggia di San Paolo, with its ten arches.

Sylvie said, "A suite—for just two of us? These rooms are huge."

"I wasn't sure," her mother said. "I didn't know if you'd want, well, privacy. If you like, we can use just one bedroom. Look at the size of that bed. We could sleep together, if you like. But it's lunchtime, let's go to the dining room. Then you can nap. The stores won't open until four, anyway. Let's get on the Italian schedule, what do you say?"

There was that awkwardness with her mother. She was oversensitive, trying too hard. She knew approximately what had happened; she had talked to the doctors and the police. Now she was being bright, cheerful, energetic. At some point, though, Sylvie would have to say, "Stop tiptoeing around it. I'm an adult—don't baby me."

But for now she let herself be led to lunch, then let herself be put down for a nap. Her parents had always overprotected her, probably because she was an only child. They'd worried when she got a hangnail or saw a piece of shit on the sidewalk. They'd hedged her in with restrictions. Therefore, at Pisa, she'd burst free.

No, that was too easy—it placed the blame outside herself. How comforting it would be to blame society, or history, or economic conditions for her behavior. In that way of thinking, even Ugo and Ruggiero hadn't been responsible; the drug culture was at fault—unemployment made them do it. Historical chains of events had inevitably put them into that van with Sylvie.

Not true. Up to a certain point, she could have said no. Instead, she'd said yes, and these were the consequences. It could have been much worse. They could've killed her, or cut off her breasts instead of her hair. But these were the consequences she would live with. She'd made the contract and would have to pay.

Late in the afternoon, they shopped in Via della Vigna Nuova and Via de' Tornabuoni. Her mother was a whirlwind. Shoes, five pairs, skirts and pants, blouses, sweaters, underwear, and nylons. She put Sylvie into plum-colored high heels, a dove gray skirt and jacket, and a white blouse. The rest of the things she ordered were sent to the hotel. Then came a shoulder bag to match the shoes, with a wallet to go inside. She tucked a sheaf of lire into the wallet. They stopped at an oculist's for dark glasses to hide her bruises, and then went to a *parrucchiere* to buy a wig. They bought two—one dark brown, the color of her own hair, the other blond, in case she wanted a change.

"Some luggage," her mother said, "and a raincoat and some jewelry. You'll need a watch."

"God almighty, Mother, stop. Enough."

"What about jeans and sneakers? Would you like a sweatshirt or one of those big knit sweaters?"

"No! Stop fussing. If I need anything else, I'll get it later."

"A hat, at least. Come along."

Sylvie tried on several. She finally chose the one her mother liked, a broad-brimmed hat with a dented crown, the same color as her bag and shoes. "Perfect," her mother said. "Now let's get a drink."

In the storefronts as they walked along, she saw reflected a woman who was not herself, someone in a fashionable suit, high heels, dark glasses, and hat. The hair was a rich chestnut color and extravagantly curled. She was taller than the tidy woman in brown who walked beside her. At a café in Piazza della Repubblica, they sat at an outside table, and her mother ordered scotch and soda. Sylvie ordered the same; it was just what a woman who looked like her would drink.

When the drinks arrived, her mother raised her glass and touched Sylvie's. "To the future," she said. "Let's forget the past and look ahead. I'm so glad we can."

"Yes," Sylvie said, "but the past . . . it happened."

"Don't think about it."

They sipped their drinks, then Sylvie said, "Is this how you see me, what you want me to be? These clothes?"

"I want you to be whatever you want to be. I want you to be happy."

Sylvie hesitated, then said, "We've never been really close, have we, Mother?"

A shadow crossed her mother's face. "Haven't we? I've always felt close to you—I've always loved you."

"I know you and Dad love me—you've shown it a thousand ways. But it seems your life is somewhere else. I know you and Dad are happy—you have a perfect marriage. But you've always seemed, well, sad somehow, even when you laugh."

She laughed now. "Sad? Why should I be sad?"

"Maybe I'm wrong. Parents are a mystery. The generations aren't supposed to understand each other, I guess. Could that be it?"

"Still, we have a lot in common," her mother said. She reached out and patted Sylvie's hand. "It's really nice to have a daughter old enough to talk to. We should talk a lot. If we're not close, let's become close. What a missed opportunity if we don't."

"You didn't have that opportunity—is that what you're thinking?"

"Among other things, yes," she said. "War—it's such a waste."

"Nonno and Nonna."

"Yes," her mother said. "Let's finish these and head back. I'm hungry, aren't you?"

Nonno and Nonna, Sylvie's grandparents, had been killed in World War II. Sylvie knew the story well. In 1942, as a precaution, they'd sent their daughter, Marta, to live with her Uncle Joe and Aunt Lisa in the hills near Perugia, and after the war, when Joe and Lisa immigrated to California, they brought Marta along. Joe and Lisa had no other children. When they died, Marta inherited the farm near Greve, not long before she married Mario Passini. Sylvie had been named for her grandmother.

At dinner she said, "They must have known the danger. Why didn't they run? They could have gone with you to Perugia, then come back after the war."

"I don't know," her mother said. "Who's to say why anyone does anything? I suppose it was a sense of responsibility. Nonno was the oldest son, it was his job to care for the farm. As it turned out, he and my mother stayed too long."

"At least they sent you away. If they hadn't, you wouldn't have met Dad, and I wouldn't be here."

Her mother laughed. "At least some good came out of it, wouldn't you say?"

"And some bad," Sylvie said. "I know, I know—we aren't supposed to talk about that."

"We can talk about anything you like," her mother said, "but let's not rush things. Let's get our feet on the ground first."

They went for a walk after dinner. It was November, but the air was warm—ice-cream weather. So they went to a *gelateria,* bought cups of *zabaglione,* and ate as they strolled around. When they got back to the hotel, Sylvie said, "I'll be up later. But take my hat—I wish you could take the wig. It's like summer tonight."

She went to a stone bench in the center of the piazza, facing the loggia. Within the circle of benches, to her left, were four or five men in a dispute. Two younger men were kicking a soccer ball back and forth. On the other benches, men and women smoked and talked in the semidark. Their voices rose and fell. It was a scene within bounds, civilized, peaceful. The men disputing gestured, but there were no threats. The two kicking the soccer ball kicked it to each other, cooperating.

She looked behind her at the church. On the upper levels of the ornate facade, pigeons roosted in long rows. Her mother would want to go to mass while they were here. Sylvie, nominally Catholic, would go with her. At home her parents went to mass every Sunday, but Mario had another faith as well. He had private rituals purely pagan. After the crush each autumn, he would take a wooden pail of the new wine into the vineyard and pour it on the ground. Of course, he fed the earth with fertilizers, he sprayed the young vines with fungicides, he followed avidly the developments in viticulture and enology, but he believed in the earth powers. He spoke of the Powers. It was the Powers he celebrated when he went to mass. He'd once told her, "The Powers are in you, too. Treat them with respect."

She'd always thought of her father as Mario, her mother as Mother. She respected them equally, loved them both, but felt closer to him than to her. He was more solid somehow, always there, like the hill that stood across the valley as she looked east from their kitchen window. Her mother, now, was less definite in outline, more general, or perhaps more than one thing at once. Was she maybe more like Sylvie, the girl who got straight A's at Stanford and then, at a finger snap, went like a lamb with Ruggiero?

Most of the benches had emptied. The soccer players had gone. Only two of the arguers remained, and they weren't arguing. A few lovers dawdled through the piazza. The hard stone bench reminded Sylvie that she had a body; she was still sore. Yawning, she stood up and walked to the hotel, then took the elevator to the third floor.

She found her in the sitting room, asleep in an armchair. The television showed three men in earnest discussion. She shut them off, started to wake her, but then stopped. Apparently, she had had her bath, washed her hair, and sat down to wait. She was wearing a blue bathrobe and, wrapped like a turban around her head, one of the hotel's white towels. Her hands rested in her lap. Where the robe parted at her knees, it exposed a flannel nightgown printed with yellow bells.

In sleep the face sagged, and just below the corners of the mouth were the folds that would bury the line of the chin one day. The mouth was a bit open. Sylvie bent to look at the fans of wrinkles at the corners of her eyes. The eyelids looked old and papery. At the inner corners of the eyes were little gummy deposits.

Sylvie shook her shoulder. The eyes opened. "Mamma, I know you won't understand this, but I went willingly, I wanted it to happen, I couldn't wait. You've never done a thing like that, but if you can imagine . . . ?"

"How do you know I haven't? Tell me."

She sat on the carpet by her mother's feet and began talking.

* * *

She slept late next morning. When she got up, the door to her mother's room was still closed. She showered, wrapped herself in a towel, and went to her room to dress. When she came out this time, there were rolls and coffee and orange juice on the table. The French door stood open and the sounds of traffic filled the room. Her mother came out then, and said, "Good morning—how do you feel?"

"Sluggish. Sort of fuzzy. We stayed up too late."

"It's the weather. It's going to rain. We should buy you a raincoat, maybe an umbrella. We have to get passport photos . . ."

They ate in silence. Her mother seemed flat, as if the rapport they'd felt last night had evaporated. She didn't look at Sylvie but off to one side or the other. Embarrassed, was she, at having a daughter who could do what Sylvie had done?

"Mother—what's past is past. It can't be helped."

Her mother glanced at her, then away. "It can't be helped, but it's not necessarily past."

After breakfast they went downstairs and out. Beneath low clouds, the air felt warm and sticky. They crossed the piazza to the loggia and then followed Via della Spada toward the center. At a shop on Via degli Strozzi, they bought Sylvie a raincoat. There was none of yesterday's enthusiasm—the sparkle had gone out of it. Her mother, preoccupied, laid out the money and they left.

Near the post office, she sat in a photo booth while her mother read the instructions. The camera flashed, and in three minutes there she was in quadruplicate, bewigged, lids drooping, shadows spreading down her cheeks. She looked as if she'd just come from a funeral.

At the Straw Market, they bought umbrellas. Her mother said, "It's getting late—let's take a cab." They walked back past the post office to a cab stand in the piazza.

In front of the American Consulate stood two uniformed guards with machine guns. Sylvie and her mother went between them and, in the lobby, stepped one by one through an electronic metal detector. A guard wearing a pistol waved them on toward a door made of thick, purplish glass. "What's going on?" Sylvie said.

"There are terrorists," her mother said.

The door lock snapped and they were let into an inner lobby, where five or six people waited in chairs. Each person held a white card with a number on it. Sylvie followed her mother to the receptionist's window, heard "Passini" and *"ambasciatore."* The words worked magic. The receptionist pointed to the second door in the lobby, and that lock snapped before they got to it. In they went to the counter where business was done. A middle-aged woman greeted them by name, gave Sylvie an application form, and accepted the photographs.

Within minutes she had her passport. Her mother said, "Now you're someone again. Without documents here, you're no one."

"Who am I?" she said. Her mother gave her a sharp glance.

They passed easily through the doors going out. On the street, they saw no taxis, so they set off walking along the Arno. "What's wrong, Mother?" she said.

"I don't know—those clothes. I can barely recognize you. Maybe we should start over."

They walked for several blocks, and at Piazza Carlo Goldoni took Via de' Fossi toward the hotel. It was a street of antique shops, with window displays of furniture, statuary, and paintings in ornate frames. Her mother gazed in at the goods as they passed.

When Santa Maria Novella came in sight, Sylvie said, "When shall we go to mass?"

Her mother said, "Sylvie, listen, there's something I want to tell you. Maybe I should've told you sooner, but who knows what the right time is? Let's go in here."

They entered the Loggia di San Paolo and continued to the end. "Up there," her mother said.

It was an incised stone plaque, high on the wall. From these something, bestial wagons, detainees, MARCH, 1944, AUSCHWITZ BUCHENWALD MAUTHAUSEN. "What is it?" she said.

"Well, this was the collection depot. Handy, close to the train station. Political detainees—that's nice. Jews, Gypsies, riffraff from all over Tuscany. Here's where they left for the cattle cars, and as it says, few returned. That part at the end—Florence remembers their sacrifice, so that liberty, independence, and justice will be certain for the future: don't you believe it. Liberty, independence, and justice are never certain."

"All right, I won't believe it."

"The point is, Sylvie, that this is where Nonno and Nonna saw Florence for the last time."

It took her a few seconds. She swallowed. "But you're Catholic."

"I married Mario."

"They were Jews? You had no right to keep it secret. How old were they?"

"David was thirty-four, Silvia only twenty-five."

"And you had me baptized Catholic! How could you do that?"

"There are reasons. Let's go sit down."

They crossed from the loggia to the piazza and found a bench facing the church. They sat down. Some of the people passing on the walks already had umbrellas up, though it wasn't yet raining. Sylvie said, "What reasons?"

"Uncle Giuseppe and Aunt Lisa were on the run, in hiding. They lived in fear. They didn't know from day to day . . . I was five years old when I went with them. What I learned there, well, it stayed with me. I developed certain habits, do you see? I learned not to tell anybody anything. Even Mario didn't know until just before we were married. It was like a hand squeezing my throat when I told him—I could barely get the words out. His Marta Cassuto, so pious at mass, was a Jew. Give Mario credit. It wasn't the worst thing he'd ever heard."

"Give me credit," Sylvie said. "Why didn't you tell me?"

Her mother lifted her hands and let them fall. "Call it fear. Lack of courage. Lack of faith in God. I couldn't trust God to protect you—I had to do it myself."

"Protect me from what? Christ, we live in America, Mother."

"That's an accident of time and place. The world is vicious, Sylvie. Don't ever forget it. There's no security anywhere."

"But you deprived me. You held back what was mine by right. It didn't work—you couldn't protect me from myself. Look what I did."

"No, look what was done to you."

Sylvie gazed off across the piazza. A priest came from the church, opened his umbrella, and strode rapidly around the front and out of sight. A light drizzle was beginning to wet the walks.

"Mother, maybe I don't understand what we're talking about. What are you telling me?"

"I was ashamed," she said. "Ashamed that such a thing happened to us, that I came from that. So I kept putting off telling you. I didn't want you to know."

"That doesn't make sense. You were a victim. It wasn't your fault."

"So Mario says, and I believe him. He's absolutely right. But even so, Sylvie, deep down—it's irrational, I know—but to be so hated . . ."

"It's raining," Sylvie said. "Let's go inside."

Her mother stopped her with her hand. "Wait, do you see what I mean?"

"I'm not sure. I know what shame is. But I wouldn't mind being hated. Let them hate me. We'll see who lasts."

"Sylvie, honey . . ."

She pulled her mother up from the bench, then took her arm. With the fingers of her right hand, she got the front edge of the wig and pulled it off. "Sylvie," her mother said.

She dropped the wig into a trash can. She tossed the dark glasses in after it. The rain felt cold on her head. Her mother, the small woman in brown, held back. But Sylvie pulled her on. She looked down at her mother and said softly, "Let them hate."

Umbrella Dance

Father Sebastiano was hurrying to say mass at Santa Maria Novella—and to beat the rain, which seemed imminent. He'd had to leave the church suddenly. One of his parishioners, dying of cancer, had sent for him and no one else to administer the last rites. It was a long walk, out past Porto al Prato, and one of those autumn storms had rolled in from the south. If he didn't make it back on time, Father Antonio would stand in for him, but Sebastiano didn't like to incur a debt.

When he emerged into the piazza, the blue-black clouds streaming over the spire made it appear that Santa Maria Novella, the great stone bulk of it, was tilting right toward him. "Parallax," he said. A drop of rain thumped on his hat, then two more drops, and then the sky broke like window glass, releasing solid water. He was drenched before he could get his umbrella up. Behind him, a sudden wind roared through the canyon of Via della Scala and flipped the umbrella inside out. His cassock, like a sail, carried him sideways while he fought to go straight ahead. His hat was gone. The umbrella had been ripped from his hands.

He had never seen a storm like this. He glanced up at the purple clouds just as lightning struck the pointed spire. Thunder cracked instantaneously, then rumbled upward. The thin metal cross atop the spire turned incandescent, became a blinding ball of light, swelling and contracting, balancing there on the peak.

He gained the door and ducked inside, into a perfect calm. In the Filippo Strozzi Chapel, to the right of the main altar, the mass was already under way. Father Antonio's sonorous voice broke into echoes in the high stone vault. Sebastiano, dripping wet, found a seat in the last pew. On the altar, the candle flames seemed honed to points. The air felt charged with electricity, as if the thick walls had absorbed the bolt and were now letting it out gradually. In the still space above the congregation, there hung a faint glow, and it lingered all during the service.

In his sermon, Antonio spoke about suffering, relating all human pain to that endured by Christ on the Cross. At the elevation of the Host, the sacring bell sounded particularly clear, ringing not like metal but crystal. During the benediction, Sebastiano sneezed.

After mass he thanked Antonio, who said, "For nothing. Don't mention it."

"Did you hear the thunder?"

"Who didn't hear it? What a bang."

"Well, it hit the spire, the cross. Did you feel it?"

"Feel it? How could I? The cross is grounded."

"Did you . . . notice anything strange during the service?"

"No, I don't think so, why?"

Sebastiano sneezed. Antonio said, "You'd better get some dry things on, or you'll land in the infirmary."

"That was a very good sermon," Sebastiano said.

There was lots he didn't understand about electrical phenomena. He wished he understood more. He had often wished he were learned in some scientific discipline, some branch of natural science, and that, assigned to a post in the Vatican, he could spend his days reconciling doctrine and the world. He enjoyed abstract thought. As a result, his sermons always had a degree of difficulty to them—too high a degree, according to some of his fellow priests, for this was a working parish. To hold this congregation's attention, one couldn't stay in the abstract for long. One had to descend, and quickly, to illustrating a text by common examples. He sometimes thought that his parishioners would have preferred examples, one story after another, like a string of fables, with no connection at all to the concept of faith.

His brother Dominicans were right—he was a working priest in a working parish, and that was his lot. There was no point in wishing to be something he wasn't. He had no scientific education, and it was too late to get it. He was fifty-six years old and too busy with his offices, with counseling, with the orphanage. Who had time to study science? There wasn't even time to meditate as much as he should have, and as for fasting, who could go three days without food while running here and there, busy every minute? This cold he felt coming on, he almost wished it would turn to flu, knock him out of action legitimately, and force him to deny the flesh for the good of the spirit.

At lunch in the rectory, he was unusually quiet. The soup, though hot, didn't taste right, the bread felt grainy but had no taste at all, and the voices around the table sounded hollow in his ears. No one else seemed to notice a strangeness in the food; therefore the strangeness was in himself, but how could a soaking and a chill tell his body to be different? Did the weather speak directly to certain organisms in his body, saying, "Grow strong"? Did everyone who'd gotten caught in that storm feel now as he felt?

That storm, too—how freakish. Though so violent and sudden that it nearly swept him away, it had released only the one thunderbolt. He didn't remember any thunder, any lightning flashing in the stained-glass windows, during the service. Who ever heard of a storm with just one flash? And that one hitting the cross, lighting it up like a fireball! Perhaps it was a sign. As far as Sebastiano knew, he was the only one who had seen this one. But perhaps others could verify it, people who'd been caught, like him, in the sudden downpour, the roaring wind in the piazza.

He would have enjoyed thinking further about these matters. He would have liked puzzling over lightning as an electrical phenomenon and as a sign from heaven. The bolt that struck Saul, had it been a natural phenomenon selected by God for His purposes, or had He distorted nature, rearranged it, for the purpose of selecting His great convert?

Sebastiano had read somewhere that, although lightning appears to strike from above, in reality the current runs the other way, toward the clouds, as the overcharged earth relinquishes her surplus. Could a sign, then, ascend? Could the ordinary world strike into the heavens? To the rational mind, that wouldn't make sense. Of course, reason could carry one only so far and no farther. He wished he had time to discuss the matter with a theologian. He could have used a few afternoons in the meteorology section of a good library, too. He remembered where he'd come across that article on lightning—it was in a popular magazine that someone had dropped in the cloister—and he'd read it in a rush, between here and there. Perhaps he hadn't understood it properly, or perhaps it hadn't been accurate to begin with.

At any rate, he couldn't think about it now. He was scheduled to hear confessions. For Sebastiano the confessional was the most painful of offices. Even those who had little on their conscience seemed to rationalize, to be hiding behind the formula of the language. It made him uneasy to have to probe with questions to ascertain the nature of the sin, and he could never determine, by the response, the true degree of contrition in the penitent's soul. And then, from time to time, something horrible came through the grille. I killed my brother, I raped the little girl next door, I murdered my best friend so as to have his wife. Confessions of this kind stunned Sebastiano like blows from a hammer. He felt his air choked off. He could barely speak. In his years here, he had heard every variety of suffering that one person could inflict upon another. The permutations of sin seemed endless, and each new variant struck terror into his soul. He had never become inured to it. Sometimes it seemed that mankind's degradation was so vast and comprehensive that even God's mercy must be at a loss. How could God care for creatures so deceptive, corrupt, and brutal?

That afternoon, near the end of his scheduled time, a folded note came through the grille. He opened the curtain for some light. The note said, "Please, before we kill ourselves, come to Via di Palombo 8, Second Floor, Nobile." The curtain on the outside was still closed. He said, "Yes? Speak." But whoever it was had gone. He stepped from the booth. There were some tourists gaping at Masaccio's *Christ Triumphant,* by the west wall, and as usual, in the left transept, there were four or five people gazing horrified at Blessed Alessio Strozzi's corpse. Perhaps the culprit had fallen in with one of those groups.

He hadn't time to investigate. Signora Montucci was waiting. He went back into the booth and drew the curtain.

Via di Palombo—Dove Street—wasn't in his parish. It was on the other side of town, near Santa Croce. Was he required to walk all the way over there, especially since he was coming down with a cold? He weighed the decision. Cold or no cold, he had to go, even though the request was outrageous. He borrowed Father Antonio's umbrella and set out. As soon as the outside air touched him, he sneezed explosively three times. He grumbled. Why hadn't they, whoever they were, gone to their own priest?

Because they didn't have one, most likely. Or if they did, they were too embarrassed to speak to him. Too embarrassed or too shifty. In Sebastiano's mind, there was no incongruity in seriousness between embarrassment and suicide. In fact, he had known people to commit suicide because they feared embarrassment. He swallowed. His throat was sore.

The rain was fine but cold. The storm had brought cold air in its wake. But the weather hadn't diminished the flow of people on the streets. As he went toward the center of town, he moved in a constant stream of umbrellas, bobbing up and down, of cars narrowly missing each other, of vehicles and pedestrians moving in all directions. Logically, there should have been an accident every few minutes, and in that crowd lots of eyes should have been put out by umbrella ribs. But he encountered no injuries. In fact, very few of the cars were scratched or dented. How was that possible? The whole moving city was like a complicated mechanical toy, the parts all interlocked and moving smoothly. There was a finite variety of vehicles, and as for the people, however they differed in appearance, they fit within the seven basic types.

There were the proud, the lustful, the slothful—the covetous, angry, gluttonous, and envious. Whatever their appearance might seem to indicate, inside they were scarred and broken, malformed, blind, twisted, and insane. No matter how attractive they might seem in their clothing, their souls were ugly and unlovable. How could God have made such creatures, have let them multiply like bacteria to despoil the lovely garden of earth?

His feet were wet again, and he'd forgotten to pick up a hat, so now his head was cold. He shivered. This time the chill seemed to have invaded his bones. By the way his eyes were blurring, he thought he must have a fever. Look where his eyes had led him: he was on the wrong street, completely turned around. Where was Santa Croce? Had he already passed it? Over in this part of town, the streets all looked alike.

He put logic to work and devised a pattern. He turned left, went three blocks, and turned right. After six blocks in that direction, he turned right again, and would have gone six blocks, ultimately covering a square six blocks by six, if, on the second leg, he hadn't found Via di Palombo. *"Ecco,"* he said, "it was there all along."

He found number 8. He pressed the button beside the name Nobile, and at once the door lock clicked. In the lobby, a heavy iron gate blocked the way to the elevator. So many locks in Florence, so many bars and security devices: half the population were thieves, the other half misers guarding their ill-gotten possessions. Mounted on one wall was a television camera. He glared at it, and the lock of the gate snapped. He pushed through and rode the elevator to the second floor.

A girl met him there. "Come in, Father," she said. "I'm Gina Nobile. This is my brother, Lorenzo. Come along." They were very young. The girl was wearing a light green skirt and a white blouse. The boy had on gray slacks and sweater. They moved gracefully, very light on their feet.

He followed them into a spacious, well-furnished living room. In fact, it was richly furnished. The kind of goods one saw in the antique shops on Via de' Fossi were everywhere in evidence here: oriental rugs, porcelain lamps, patterned upholstery on the couches and chairs. There were paintings and tapestries on the walls, and, on the mantel over the marble fireplace, a row of small bronze sculptures that must have been worth a fortune. These people were wealthy.

They took him through to a smaller sitting room and offered him a chair. They sat together on a love seat. At the ends of the love seat stood identical ceramic table lamps, with figures in bas-relief, a procession of satyrs and nymphs following each other in a dancing circle.

He said, "Well, my name is Sebastiano. What can I do for you?" He shifted in his chair a little and crossed his legs. In one motion, they crossed their legs, too, and folded their hands in their laps.

It was the girl who led off. "Our father died ten years ago—Emiliano Nobile. Have you heard of him?"

"Who hasn't?" Sebastiano said. "Though I understand that mass is said for him at Santa Croce."

They didn't pick up the implied question: why therefore did you come to me? Instead, the boy said solemnly, "Yes, he endowed the church substantially in his will. He left his family well-off, as you can see. These things were all his. Now they're ours. We have, really, quite a lot of money."

"We? What about your mother?"

The girl said, "She died last April, was killed, rather, in a plane crash. It was in the newspapers."

"I seldom read the news. But who looks after you now?"

"We look after ourselves," the boy said. "There's the cook and the housekeeper, but we take care of ourselves and each other."

"How old are you?"

In unison they said, "Twenty."

Sebastiano glanced around the room. On a stand by one wall was a bronze statue of Venus and Cupid—an entanglement of arms and legs, obscene and expensive. On the opposite wall a tapestry depicted Leda with a gigantic swan. At the center of the third wall hung a picture of Saint Teresa in ecstasy—in sexual ecstasy: it wasn't her heart she guided the angel's lance to. By the way the thing was lighted, he guessed it must be a treasure. How could a thing be a treasure and still be worthless?

With distaste he said, "There doesn't seem to be much reason for killing yourselves. Or was that note just a practical joke?"

"I'm pregnant," the girl said.

Sebastiano sighed. His throat felt scratchy. There was a marked tightness in his chest. He said, "I take it the cook is not the father."

"No, the cook is a woman," the boy said, and Sebastiano could have laughed. The boy said earnestly, "We love each other."

Sebastiano coughed around an obstruction in his throat. The girl said, "Would you like some tea?"

"No, no. Thank you," he said. "You're sure about this?"

"Absolutely," the girl said. The boy nodded.

Sebastiano's teeth ached. He clenched them together and the pain went to his cheekbones.

"You are very beautiful," he said, "and very stupid. Here you have all that the material world can offer, you could live like angels here, and you have to do a stupid thing like that. Then on top of it, you want to kill yourselves, eh?"

"But what if the child turns out an idiot?" the boy said. "There's a good chance of it, you know. We could go to Sweden for an abortion. That's what our lawyer recommends. But we think we want the child. It's a child made in love."

"So, then, you don't want to kill yourselves."

"We don't want to have to," the girl said. "But we might have no choice. We could do it, you see—we could put an end to everything. We love each other, really past understanding, and we could just leave the world together, all three of us."

"You're Catholic?"

"Oh yes," they said together, and the girl added, "Not very good Catholics."

"No question about that," he said. "Let's see, to the crime of incest—it's a crime by law, as well as a sin—you would add the sin of self-murder and that of murdering your unborn child, which is also a crime. If you were to have an abortion, there would be only the murder. Or you could avoid all those murders. You could get married, have your baby, and live happily, though the baby would probably be defective, and neither the Church nor the state would allow brother and sister to marry."

"We could marry in Mexico or Sweden," said the boy. "We've thought about it. It could be done."

"Oh yes, the money—I forgot about the money. With money you can do anything, except save your immortal souls. Do you have some aspirin?"

They got up together, the girl and the boy, and left the room. They were children, a young Adam and Eve playing in the Garden. Mustn't touch. So, of course, that's the first thing they did. And now the agony, God's absence, the blindness, the corrupt condition of the natural life here on earth. From him, what did they want—spiritual help? Not a bit of it. They wanted counseling, some way out of the mess.

The girl brought the aspirin on a saucer, the boy a glass of mineral water on another. He swallowed the pills. They hurt going down and even the water stung his throat. "Are you sorry for what you did?" he said.

"We did it," said the boy. "We take responsibility for it. Besides, the child might be a genius. That sometimes happens."

He groaned. "A genius? Are you two geniuses? You're geniuses at being stupid."

"Is love stupid?" the girl asked. "I thought love was the best thing there is. I know ours is very fine—isn't it, Lorenzo?"

"We were lovers in the womb, I think," said the boy.

The aspirin seemed to have brought on a headache. He felt dead tired. This was so hopeless that, if he'd had the energy, he would have flung the bronze Venus through a window. "Lovers in the womb, indeed," he said. "Well, lovers, I suggest you take your lawyer's advice. You, little girl, get an abortion—and you go with her, hold her hand. And then one of you go to the North Pole, one to the South Pole, and never see one another again. Do your loving at a distance, by mail. See how long love lasts under those conditions. And get back into Mother Church. Confess and never cease confessing. You are guilty, guilty, guilty." He put his hand to his cheek. "Just do what your lawyer tells you. Now I must go, I'm sick."

He got up and hurried to the door, and the beautiful, self-befouled children followed. He didn't say good-bye, he shut the door behind him, took the elevator down, and burst past the security arrangements. In the street, he groaned with relief as the rain cooled his head—with relief at being out of that animals' den. "Love," they'd said—but they were animals.

He cooled a little, then more than a little, and he realized that he'd left his umbrella back there. Worse, in anger, in a frenzy of hopelessness, he had forgotten his priestly office. He had advised those children to commit murder. What did a priest deserve who so far forgot himself as to accept complicity in a crime—worse than a crime? He'd plunged himself into a state of sin.

Every time he put a foot down, his leg shook. He tucked his hands into his armpits and hugged himself. His body jerked this way and that. "Good," he said, "burn up, fall apart, devour yourself."

But by the time he reached the Duomo, he was no longer flagellating himself. He had to lie down or fall in the street. The cathedral was closed. Across the street was the Misericordia, where he could find help, but he couldn't get there; he felt faint; he would never make it. How embarrassing it would be to fall to the pavement, and he a priest. To his right, the doors of the Baptistery stood open. From somewhere he found strength. He stumbled inside and fell on the step by the old baptismal font, then blacked out.

When he came to himself, he saw how he'd gotten in. Ghiberti's doors were almost never open—Michelangelo had called them the Gates to Paradise—but tonight a team of photographers had them open, floodlighting the lower panels, setting up the tripod for the camera. Because he was a priest, they hadn't stopped him.

Inside the pointed dome, lights came on, and other photographers began setting up long-lensed cameras to take the high, storytelling sequences of mosaics. Sebastiano sat there; no one bothered him; they were all too busy jumping to the shouted orders of the man in charge, a bearded young man in a leather jacket. His shouts echoed off the walls and bounced around in the huge space. He wanted Christ first, the whole panel and then the details. He pointed with his finger, and Sebastiano followed with his eyes and saw the familiar *Christ the Judge of the World*, consigning with His left hand sinners to hell, raising with His right the ranks of the blessed.

The director called for lights, and at once the figure leaped into brilliance on the sloping ceiling. The background of gold, made of thousands of tiny mosaics, glittered unevenly, seemed to undulate in waves, and Christ Himself, standing out against the background, moved in and out, swelling and contracting, radiating superb light. Each minuscule stone was a point of brilliance, in itself steady, and yet the whole configuration moved, responding to the great light flowing out from Christ. In the highest rank of the saved, the saints, he saw Saint Sebastian, whose name he'd taken upon being ordained, moving and glittering among the others.

Thousands of mosaics, no, millions, billions—for the scenes depicted on the ceiling encompassed the history of the world from Creation to Destruction. Billions of atoms in perfect fit, all moving in coherent arrangement, from beginning to end.

He got up and went outside. His shaking had stopped; he wasn't sick anymore. The rain falling on his head was warm, like a mist in late spring, good for the crops. Umbrellas bobbed as before, never quite touching, and, as before, the traffic moved, the people moved, in a complicated arrangement by which each person had a modicum of space, though all were together. The stones of the buildings fitted neatly, and the buildings in a close fit made streets and blocks of streets. The paving stones fitted attractively at angles to each other, shining wetly in the light from streetlamps and shops.

It was beautiful. All the faces were smiling. Streams of people moving in opposite directions simply flowed through one another, umbrellas tilting to the left, to the right, bobbing, bowing, never quite touching. Sebastiano smiled at everyone he met. What warmth, what perfection!

That lightning bolt this morning, what was it but God's grace given to the church, to be distributed in small doses where there was need. Oh, there was need! The scarred, the broken, the spiritless—those imprisoned in themselves, those without love or with the wrong kind of love: the two children he'd talked to, and himself, chief among sinners. Christ's warm rain entered him drop by drop until he overflowed, gave back from the abundance.

He kicked out a foot, and then the other one, as umbrellas danced around him. The lost, the troubled, the self-torturers and those tortured by others, and yes, the killers and rapists, they were all God's children; His light shone on them all! His rain washed away their sins.

He made his way to the rectory, discarding his sins as he went, growing lighter with each step.

In the hallway, he met Antonio, whose eyes grew large. "Sebastiano, what happened? Where are your clothes? Oh, you're like a furnace! A blanket, someone, hurry!"

They surrounded Father Sebastiano and wrapped him in blankets, then hurried him off to the infirmary.

The Pleasures
of the Senses

Gino Fuori lived in a *fondo,* a basement apartment, and so, unlike most people, he had to climb up into the world every morning to go to work. He would have climbed a lot farther, labored hand over hand up a rope, to escape. So many children down there, such squabbling! The smells! It was a warren they lived in. They lived like foxes in a den. Five little ones, and Natalia not yet thirty. Well, that's what you got when you married one of those round, succulent ones: a factory. She'd gone to fat, too, so now where was he?

At the top of the stairs, he stepped into Via del Moro and took a breath of fresh air. Ah, a fine autumn morning, one of those November Saturdays that warm gradually, when girls take off their clothing layer by layer until their nipples show. There would be a football game that afternoon, Florence against Verona, with some forty thousand nipples in the stadium. To see that many nipples, he would crawl across town on hands and knees. He would scale the wall with his fingernails.

He adjusted his hat, drew his chin in, and sauntered like a Spanish aristocrat into Piazza Santa Maria Novella. There were already lots of people on the sidewalks, at least half of them women. There went two priests scurrying to the church like rats for a hole, but behind them was a group of nuns. Nuns could be good, sometimes very good—all that trapped passion exploding like a volcano. Oh, look, look at that one, that girl on the bicycle, legs pumping, face gone in a trance, the horn of the seat right up in there, working back and forth between her legs. Lucky seat! Wouldn't he horn her, though? Wouldn't he stir her little cup of honey?

He took his morning coffee at a bar on the piazza. Though he knew what he would see, he looked at the mirror to see again. The wide-brimmed Spanish hat, the concave cheeks so smoothly shaved, the sharp, strong nose, and the hot Spanish eyes: he'd left the hacienda that morning to inspect the new shipload of Circassian slaves. He would buy a dozen or so to help around the house. He tilted his head a little and watched the hot Spaniard drink his coffee. He wore his coat like a cape around his shoulders. It gave him a look of casual elegance, indifference, until one noticed the smoldering eyes.

It also partially concealed the cane, which he sported carelessly, like an affectation, pretending he didn't need it. But he did need it. When he walked, there was no concealing the unnatural bend in his leg and the heavy, sloping shoe on his right foot. When he was twelve, a building stone had dropped from an overhead scaffold, caromed off a coping, and smashed his knee in sideways. It had healed at an angle, and the lower part had stopped growing. He wore a knee brace, too, but it was concealed by his pants. He preferred standing to walking, since he could stand without limping, but when he had to walk, he kept his back straight and head erect, relying on style to draw attention upward to his hot, handsome face.

He walked past the church and took the pedestrian underpass to the train station. There he descended the stairs to the Albergo Diurno, the day hotel where travelers, waiting between trains, could refresh themselves. They could rent a cot and rest, have a shower, enjoy a massage. Those whose hair had gone wild could have it tamed by the hairdresser. They could eat and drink at the bar, or be served at the tables, and at the shop they could buy a toothbrush, lotions, razor blades, mouthwash, underwear, socks —the small personal things that travelers often want. If their shoes were smudged, Gino would shine them.

He hung his coat and hat carefully on a peg in the cubicle behind his stand. He rolled back his shirt cuffs, then brought out an assortment of brushes, rags, creams, waxes, and liquid polishes. He attached the brass footrest to the bracket in the floor. He put his low stool in place and dusted the high leather chair, the seat shiny from the pants, sometimes the skirts, of hundreds of patrons over the years. Most of his customers were men, who tipped well for good service, but the occasional woman was in herself a gratuity, and he would have done her for nothing.

So far this morning, there were neither men nor women, so he went to the bar for his second cup of coffee and passed the time with Aldo Riccardi, the chief of the underground domain. Aldo's passion was football. He invested heavily in the state football pools and kept a book of the bets he made on the side. Today he offered Gino Florence, for ten thousand lire, against Verona, and Gino snapped it up. It was the politic thing to do, since Aldo had the power to hire and fire. If by a miracle Florence should win, it would be money in his pocket. If not, it was the cost of doing business.

His first three customers were men. Gino took a leave of absence and let his hands do the job. But then came a lovely pair of boots, dark brown, with nylons and a short plaid skirt. His soul ran to his fingertips. He lifted one of the boots onto the footrest, the knees separated, and there in the shadows slept heaven's gate. As above, so below. He looked up into her face and knew, by the full moist lips, what the gate would feel like, going through. Her lips parted—oh!—and she spoke. "I'm sorry—they're quite a mess, aren't they?"

"No matter, signorina," he said. With the rough brush, he removed the dust and dirt, then quickly sealed the sole with liquid polish. This was quality footwear. He touched the scuffs with dark brown wax, smoothing it in with his thumb, and then, with one hand on her calf to steady her, he rubbed cream into the leather, with gentle, circular strokes. The cream was white; it vanished into the leather as he rubbed, and he applied more, changed hands, and began the great, long strokes on the uppers, all the way to the top, up, down, up and down. With the hand holding her calf, he felt the muscles tensing and relaxing to meet the pressure. He did a thorough job of it; he finished her off, then wiped her with the soft brush, then the rag, and looked up into her eyes. "Beautiful," he said.

He saw that she liked being above him, looking down, while he worked from below. "Another?" he said, and she set one foot down and put the other up, revealing a different view of the shadowed pass to bliss. This time he worked more slowly, lingering over the strokes, drawing out the pleasure. If she liked being in control, fine—let her think she was in control. But underneath there, where it counted, he made her do what she loved doing. Working more methodically, he made a better job of it this time, so he commanded her to put the first foot up again for a few strokes of the flannel.

"Satisfied?" he said.

"Perfectly," she said, and gave him two thousand lire. A five-hundred-lire tip? Yes. She stepped out of the seat and said, "Thank you."

"The pleasure is mine, signorina," he said.

She was wonderful, yes, but she was the only woman he had all morning. He could have used a hundred. Lots of women came down to the Diurno, but not for shoeshines; they took care of that at home, did it for themselves, to save money. It was infuriating. His name, Fuori, meant outside, and outside he remained, trying to get in. He should have been named Fuoco, fire, for he was on fire day and night, and not for fat Natalia, who didn't like it, who lay like a tub of tripes, as wide open as a church door, with nothing inside that a man could feel.

There were half a million people in Florence, at least half of them women. Take away those too old and too young, take away the crazy, diseased, and crippled, and that left easily one hundred thousand sweet, tight women on the loose. What he wouldn't do with a hundred thousand women! In hotels, under bushes, in their own beds, on pavements, tables, floors, the ground: he wanted them all! He would fall on them where they walked, nail them before they hit the earth, two, four, six at a time.

At one o'clock he put his equipment away and closed the shop. He put on his coat and hat. "See you tomorrow, Aldo," he said. Aldo laughed and said, "Bring your money. It's Verona all the way."

He had the afternoon off. He climbed the stairs painfully, but just at the top he saw one in white stockings, all knees and elbows —too young, but she would grow. Then came one in tight white pants, the crotch showing the outline of parted lips. "Oh!" he said, but immediately one appeared whose short legs were plump as pears, joining at the flower bed where, hidden, lay the sensitive red bud.

Young married ones were best, quicker to receive and not yet jaded, so that he could teach their imaginations to soar, show them what they hadn't dreamt existed, and they in turn could teach their husbands, keeping happiness in the family. But the unmarried ones, so tight they had to be forced a little, they were best, too. Those tipping toward middle age, those rising from childhood into youth, and the infinite variety of those in between: they were all best. Not one was inferior to all the others.

At a trattoria, he sat down to have pasta and wine. Eating was one of the things he did quickly, like shaving and using the toilet, to have the more time free for love. But today, as he forked spaghetti into his mouth, two tourists came in, a boy and girl, Germans. Some Germans were dark-haired, but these two had the blue-eyed, blond look almost of Swedes. How long had it been? It seemed forever since he'd tasted such young, salty lips. He pulled the curtain between boy and girl, then said softly, "Fräulein?" Why yes, she would love to see the Diurno. No matter that it was late at night. Oh, a massage table, with a motor to make it vibrate. She loved vibrations, great or small. They spent the night there, and the motor never stopped.

The weather was warmer than he'd expected, almost balmy, and the streets were crowded with breasts, buttocks, waists, hips, and legs—all different, all in motion. Sometimes variety alone could cause pain. How to choose? He encountered a pair of eyes so moist and sensual he could have licked them. Then that girl on the moped, chestnut hair flowing out behind: he could have flown beside her, his tongue in her ear, sipping nectar. He stopped at a narrow corner where two could barely pass together. He leaned and a breast brushed his shoulder, then the other breast. Ah, widely separated. He liked them far apart; he liked them close together; he liked them hanging heavily and standing straight out, with nipples on top like flounder's eyes, nipples attacking through a blouse, nipples gazing reflectively at the pavement.

If he were invisible now, he would get his hands under two skirts at once, tickling, gripping, probing, and wouldn't they weaken and forget to walk, when they learned he had more than fingers to work with? That redheaded one there, a foreigner, why not wait in the closet of her hotel room until she was fast asleep, then slip in beside her and turn the snake loose? She would think it a dream, a harmless dream snake playing between her legs, but when she woke and saw the enormous thing, how her eyes would roll! What rapture!

The bus to the stadium was packed. He wriggled into the middle of the crowd, one hand on his hat, the other fending with his cane, and stopped when he couldn't move farther. The driver shouted, "Move forward!" The crowd surged from behind, no one ahead gave way, and he got his hands down just in time, for when the door closed, and again the crowd surged, they pressed together in a force fit. His good leg had lodged between hers, and he felt her abdomen pressing just below his own. Her breasts he was deprived of, for she clutched her purse over them with both hands.

When the bus started, bodies shifted and jiggled like a truckload of grapes. There was no danger of losing balance; no one could move, a person could die in there and not fall over. Gino's hat had slid a little forward, but he couldn't get a hand up to straighten it. The bus turned a corner and she pressed harder against him. She lifted her eyes to his face. *"Scusi,"* she said.

What eyes they were! What a honey-smooth, tawny complexion! Sicilian, was she? That thick dark hair, a mouth to make the devil shriek, to melt pebbles, to suck a priest away to destruction! The pressure on his thigh: Venus' hill? He moved his hand a little. She raised her eyes and looked right at him. He moved and she drew her breath sharply. She tried pulling back but couldn't, and anyway he had a grip now.

She took her lower lip between her teeth. She looked away, pretending she didn't notice, but she noticed the thumb all right. There, wasn't she giving a little? She was! She was responding, pushing against his hand. Her eyes grew sleepy, she let herself go, and her soft lips pursed sweetly.

She spat in his face. He couldn't get his hands up to wipe it off. She spat twice more.

At the stadium, the bus doors opened and the crowd streamed forth, sweeping him along. The woman was ahead of him. She had a lascivious tail that showed the outline of skimpy underpanties. He bounded after her, whacked her buttocks with his cane, and said, "You like to spit, do you? Well, how do you like this?" He whacked her harder. She crouched in the bushes, whimpering. "Please don't hurt me anymore, oh, please." But he was relentless, he was the judge. "Oh, Judge, stop," she said. She cowered, limp, his to do with as he wished. He did and did and did.

His ticket was for a seat near the Verona goal, but about halfway to the top. By the time he'd climbed up there, his leg was aching, and then he found himself between a large woman with hairs on her chin, whose husband looked like an arm breaker for the Camorra, and an effeminate little man with a lisp. Right in front of him was a nice head of hair, but as he was taking a fistful, turning the head around, and pulling the face into his lap, he realized it was a wig. He hadn't even completed her face—eager mouth, helpless eyes—when her hair turned false. The picture fell apart.

There were mostly men around him, and worse, they were a mixture of Florentines and Veronese, so the predominating mood was warlike. Gino didn't care for war; it was distracting; it interfered with the finer things in life. On the field, it was warfare pure and simple, as men whose legs were unbelievably packed with muscle ran, kicked, leaped, and sacrificed their bodies to put the ball past the goalie. If Gino had legs like that, he wouldn't waste them chasing a ball.

Fiaschi of wine circulated among friends, and *fiaschetti* of brandy appeared. The crowd lost its mind. People shook their fists, chanted in unison, cheered, whistled derisively. A few rows down, a fight broke out and the security guards dragged two men and a woman to the exit. People were descending to the level of animals. He found the spectacle disgusting.

Then late in the final period, a fine rain began falling. The bearded woman to his right opened an umbrella, but she shared it with her brutish husband, which left Gino no alternative but to

duck under the little pervert's umbrella. It was unpleasant rubbing shoulders with him, and he tried avoiding contact between
their legs, but if he wanted to keep his hat dry, he had to pay the
price. The little fellow kept touching him as if by accident, rounding his eyes and mouth in astonishment, and fluttering his fingers
like a helpless girl.

It was a foul afternoon. Verona won, two goals to nothing. He
owed Aldo ten thousand lire. The bus to the station was as packed
as the one coming out, but this time he was caught between two
drunken men who argued across him and blew stale wine into his
face.

When he got off at the station, the rain was heavier. Night had
fallen prematurely. There were lights behind the stained-glass
windows of Santa Maria Novella. Heat lightning flashed in the
clouds, as a storm moved ponderously in from the south. His knee
ached—it always ached in rainy weather—and despite precau-
tions his hat had gotten wet. With a choice between going home
and not, he started off toward the city center.

Rain or shine, there were always people on the streets, half of
them women. More by habit than design, he touched a few as he
went along, though their raincoats put an extra unfeeling layer
between flesh and flesh. With rain coming down hard, he couldn't
break the barrier and strip them, couldn't take them into alleys,
lobbies, sacristies for the fucking they deserved. In Borgo San
Lorenzo, he went into a self-serve restaurant to rest his leg. He
bought a bowl of ravioli and a glass of wine. His spirits rose as he
watched two young lesbians at the table next to him. They
tongued one another, he came between them with his own tongue,
and then he introduced them to something that made them forget
tongues.

It didn't work well, and besides, they left. A middle-aged
woman took their place. She was well dressed but owned the kind
of face where all the lines lead downward. She'd seen too much,
done too much. Sex was but a dream for her by now, an after-

thought. More in despair than joy, he took her anyway. She was capacious and inert. She flapped open like a dry cistern, a vault full of bones and skulls. He couldn't stir life into the old hulk.

She ate and departed. Two priests came in. Gino left.

On Via degli Strozzi, he stopped at a boutique to watch a woman undressing a manikin. She took the sweater off, then the skirt. When the bra came off, the breasts just stood there eyeless, and the crotch turned out to be plain joints. Gino couldn't do a thing with it. The window dresser, a no-nonsense woman with short hair and square hands, didn't yield much, either. He tried to interject something to break her down, but in a businesslike way she drew a nightgown over the dummy. She adjusted the limbs, draped the garment to her satisfaction, and then bent to retrieve the discarded clothing. As she stooped, her sweater rode up in back, exposing a strip of flesh that had hair on it. Gino extrapolated—he couldn't help it—and turned away from buttocks and thighs as furry as a goat's.

A block farther along, he ducked under an awning outside a gallery. In the window was perhaps the thousandth Madonna and Child he'd seen in the city. He looked her over. He could sometimes get it going with the Virgin. But this one, with a syrupy holier-than-thou innocence on her face, was no Virgin. Some husky farm boy had stuck her behind the barn. She'd told her impotent old husband that God did it, and he believed her. Gino tried halfheartedly to pork her himself, but he couldn't get her off the canvas, and the chubby kid wouldn't go away.

His coat was soaked through. Water dripped from the brim of his hat. What a day! He'd had only one good one, and she'd spat in his mouth. Now lightning was flashing, thunder booming in the streets, and the rain had become a downpour. To hell with it. He was ruined anyway, so he walked into the thick of it, in the center of the street.

In Piazza Santa Maria Novella, lightning lit up the facade of the church, made it leap forward a few feet at every flash. Water swirled around his feet. The gutters couldn't hold it all. There was no one in the piazza except himself. As he watched, a bolt struck the metal cross atop the church spire, and at the same instant thunder cracked. The air smelled of electricity. He spat. "Hit me —go ahead!" he shouted. He held his cane aloft for a target.

He kept the cane in the air, though he had to drag his foot, as he went the two blocks to Via del Moro. He came to his door. Before going in, he spat in the foaming gutter. He looked along the street toward the river. "Rise, you bastard—flood us out!"

But he let himself in quietly, and made as little noise as possible going downstairs. Let sleeping dogs lie.

He hung his dripping hat and coat on the rack. God, it stank down there. Grease, old food, bodies. He took off his shirt and flung it. He flung his undershirt. He caned his way into the dark bedroom and sat on the bed. She didn't stir, but he could smell her, a beached whale beside the nighttime sea.

He unlaced his heavy shoe and got it off. He removed the other shoe. They were soaked. He got out of his wet pants, shorts, and socks, leaving them on the floor. Even the leather brace was soaked. He unlaced it and let it drop. Rubbing the bent, scarred knee, digging his thumbs into it, he sat in the dark. "Fucking leg," he said. "Holy Mary Mother of God, what a life."

She was mountainous, but warm. He slid up next to her. In the children's room, one of them cried out, shrieked, howled like a dog. She moved her arm and said, "What?" The howling ceased.

"Polpa," he said, "are you awake?" It was the nickname he'd given her when they were married, when she was like the flesh of a just-ripe pear, so full and sweet.

"Gino?" she said sleepily.

"Who else would it be?" he said.

Then he clambered up and got on her.

Massimo

Ho, what a morning! He had barely swallowed his coffee when the crowd swept in, rushing for the early train to Rome, and that train, from Bologna, disgorged as many passengers as it took on. Out to the street he went, his hand truck loaded with bags, then in to the platform, loaded again. Good service, good tips!

Businessmen, tourists, students, whole families—people of all descriptions arriving, departing—it was that way all morning. So many travelers! You'd think Florence was the center of the world! But the faces—nothing but frowns today, angry noses and chins, and elbows jabbing this way and that as if a gold coin were hidden somewhere and everyone had to find it.

Well, that was their affair. His was to make conversation, to find empty compartments and hoist bags in through the windows, to find taxis, give directions, suggest a restaurant or hotel, and show foreigners how to use the pay telephones. He was a welcoming committee, a bon voyage party, a calming influence. Unless they were misers, people tipped him well. If they were misers, curse them. They lived their punishment and would die all pinched up.

The trick was to hurry while giving the impression of leisure. He pretended he had nothing to do all day but care for the ones he was dealing with at the moment, but for all his chatter he moved right along, to be rid of one bunch and latch onto the next. "Hello, I'm all yours, good-bye!"

He made a living. He sometimes got a little extra, a gift from God, as had happened that morning when a rich American and his wife stepped off the train from Pisa. They owned big leather suitcases and carried pressed raincoats over their arms. Their faces were the kind that say, "What smells bad?" They try not to touch things, that kind. They don't talk or smile.

They don't like lines, either, so Giuseppe wedged them in first at the taxi stand. "Four bags, four thousand lire," he said. The man laid a fifty-thousand-lira note on his hand. Giuseppe started to make change, but the man brushed him away, a great lord annoyed by a gnat.

A forty-six-thousand-lira tip? Wait, sir, you've made a mistake! The taxi sped off. Well, thank you, sir! But then a dark thought: what if the man should return, complain to the Capo that Giuseppe had shortchanged him? At sixty he was the oldest of the porters; a complaint or two and the Capo could snap his fingers, replace him with someone younger.

A German would complain. A Frenchman would have counted his change in the first place. An American, though, would rather swallow his loss than create a fuss, especially since the mistake was his own. Giuseppe was almost certain of it.

At twelve-fifteen, he parked his hand truck and strode to the Capo's office. He strode because it was important to cut a good figure, no matter how his bones ached from the morning's work. It was important, too, to speak respectfully to the Capo, who was only thirty-five and full of his responsibilities. Never ruffle a boss who thinks highly of himself, as if there were any other kind. Giuseppe said, "Permission to leave, sir? It's my afternoon off." The Capo glanced at him, then nodded.

Well now, good-bye, sir. He left the station, crossed the street, and went straight to the doll store. With some of his found money, he bought a pretty, yellow-haired girlfriend for his son. Other boys had girlfriends—why not his son as well? With the doll in his pocket, he hurried to the elementary school. Ah, he was on time. He stood among other parents waiting for their children.

The bell sounded and the double doors opened out. Then the children came like leaves with an autumn wind behind them, carrying their little satchels, calling good-bye to one another, good-bye to their teachers. What sweet, clear voices! The teachers led the special children by the hand and turned them over personally to their parents. Giuseppe received Massimo from Signora Rondelli, who said, "Wednesday again, eh, Giuseppe?"

"Say good-bye, Massimo," he said. He took the boy from the courtyard into Via della Scala and steered him along. "Pigeons," he said, but the boy preferred the things to the word. What did "pigeons" mean, unless there were real birds to touch? When they came into Piazza Santa Maria Novella, though, didn't his face light up? There were a thousand pigeons strutting and pecking, their feathers giving off light. When Massimo went gently among them, doing his dance, didn't they recognize him and gather round? They climbed all over him. He chortled and cooed, and all you could see was birds, no Massimo.

But a truck backfired and all the wings went at once. Massimo gazed at the swirl of their going, his face radiant, feathers falling in the air around him.

To get his attention, Giuseppe offered the doll, and soon they were walking hand in hand along Via dell'Inferno. At Via del Purgatorio, their street, they turned right. These streets were ancient and narrow, not the best place in the world to raise a family, but everyone had to live somewhere. It happened that they lived there. At their door, he rang the bell to let Maria know they were coming, and then he swung Massimo in long leaps up the four flights of stairs.

She met them in the living room. "Look at the dirt," she said.

"Pigeons," he said. "Clothes can be washed. What shall we do today? What's the plan?"

"Another doll? He'll just tear it up."

"He doesn't mean to," Giuseppe said. "He forgets."

The soup was ready. While Maria filled the bowls, he took Massimo to the bathroom for a wash. He said, "How was school today? You outshone them all, eh? For a treat, let's go to the park, play in the grass. We'll take the bus and watch the houses."

Soup was difficult for him. Maria tried getting him to dip his bread in, then eat the bread, but he liked the spoon. The towel around his neck didn't catch all he spilled. In spite of herself, she got cross: "Massimo, please try." So Giuseppe took over. "Here, like this," he said, and with the boy's fist inside his own, he guided the spoon to the mouth.

After lunch came nap time. Giuseppe removed the heavy shoes, undressed him, released the brace. He covered him and put the doll in the crook of his arm. He talked him to sleep with the story of the foolish American.

In the kitchen, Maria had cleaned up the mess and was sitting at the table, holding her head. Things were harder on her than on him. Except when the boy was in school, she was with him every second until Giuseppe came home, and he worked long hours. To have raised four and seen them grown, and then to have this one come along in her old age—no wonder she was discouraged.

"Let's have a glass of wine," he said, "then lie down awhile."

The wine raised her spirits a little. As they lay side by side on the bed, then, she related the morning's news. There had been two letters, one from Gina, in Orvieto—she was pregnant again, with her third—and one from Enzo, in Verona. Enzo wanted them to install a telephone, at his expense, so he could call and talk once in a while. "A loving son," Giuseppe said. "Why couldn't Roberto offer a telephone?"

Roberto, the oldest, was thirty-eight. He seldom wrote. He was a lawyer in Rome, divorced, a playboy. Giuseppe remembered how, even as a child, he'd been quick to receive, slow to give. For some reason, maybe because he was the firstborn, Maria favored him. Giuseppe's favorite among the first four was Elisabetta, the youngest, the closest to Massimo in disposition. But she lived with her husband in London, a city too far away to think about.

"What will happen to him when we die?" Maria said.

"We won't die. God wouldn't let us, with him to care for. Don't worry about it."

"What if you hurt your back again, and can't work?"

"My back is a pillar. I could lift the bed with you in it, and throw the wardrobe on, too, for good measure."

"Don't joke, Giuseppe. Last time, you went five years without work."

"Didn't God repair me? Didn't he send Massimo? Who would have guessed you could conceive, a woman past bearing? No one would believe it. God will take care of his gift, you can bet on that."

At three o'clock, the boy began making his noise, a low howl interspersed with chirps and yelps. Giuseppe went in to get him ready. He gathered the yellow hair from the bedclothes, from the boy's mouth. He said, "Ho, ho, Massimo, let's go find the bus!"

At ten years old, he was really too heavy to swing between them as they went downstairs, but since he loved swinging, they did it. At the bottom, he wanted to go up for another ride. Maria groaned. Giuseppe caught his eye with what was left of the doll.

On the bus, they sat him by the window, and Maria sat beside him. As the world moved beyond the glass, he started singing. Giuseppe, standing in the aisle, squeezed Maria's shoulder. "Let him," he said. Other passengers craned around to see where the sound was coming from. Never mind them! The boy's face twisted with pleasure as he sang to the sliding world.

At the park, he headed off across the green lawn, dancing as he went. He took long, slow steps at an angle, as always when no one steered him, and then interrupted himself with ecstatic jerks, as if his arms were on wires. Giuseppe said, "Look at that—where does he think he's going?" Maria suddenly laughed—she couldn't help herself—and kicked one of her legs out a little. "Hey, Grandmother," Giuseppe said, and did a few cavorting steps back and forth.

Massimo plunged into a bush and disappeared. In that drawn-out, sweet voice of hers, Maria called, "Massimo—here we are." He emerged rolling and kept rolling until Giuseppe caught him up, held him high, and whirled him around.

"Grass stains," Maria said. "We should buy him all green clothes."

There were other children in the park, but none like Massimo. The others ran faster and went where they aimed themselves, but they bickered and contested and pouted like little adults. Not so Massimo. All by himself, he sang, rolled, and danced. The park was his world. The park was perfect. He couldn't have asked for more.

They kept an eye on him from a bench. Now and then, Giuseppe jumped up to head him off when he doubled back toward the street. They gave him the whole afternoon, and even then he would have stayed, crawled under a shrub to sleep, but Giuseppe led him with the doll to the bus. Then the world began sliding in the opposite direction.

From the bus stop, they walked toward Via del Purgatorio in the October dusk. Giuseppe said, "I just remembered something. You go ahead, I'll catch up."

He turned into an alley and cut through to Via del Parione. At a florist's, he bought a huge bouquet of chrysanthemums, and at a sweetshop, a great, round box of chocolates. He hurried home, then, to be waiting at the door.

In time they came along. Maria said, "Candy? Flowers? Where did the money come from?"

He exchanged the presents for Massimo, lifted him to his shoulder, and swept him upstairs.

They had sausages and beans for dinner, and afterward they let the boy choose a chocolate. His hand dove right for the center of the box. "A geometrician, a genius," Giuseppe said, "and only half awake!"

It was true, his eyes were drooping—the exercise and fresh air had done him in. Giuseppe undressed him, unlaced the brace, and helped him at the toilet. He gave him a bath. He put his nightclothes on, covered him up in bed, and had barely begun a story about the Capo and the big fast trains when Massimo fell asleep.

"Now," Maria said, "where did you get the money?"

He told her about the rich American.

"They'll fire you," she said. "You'll get caught."

"How can they fire me? I do more work than anyone. Without me, why, the Capo would have to carry bags himself."

"It was dishonest," she said.

"Wait, now—God sent me the American. He reached out and created one who couldn't tell fifty thousand from five thousand. He sent him straight to me. Are you calling God dishonest?"

"But you spent it all on candy and flowers. You're hopeless, Giuseppe. You're worse than Massimo."

"Have a candy," he said.

They didn't stay up long. Tomorrow would come early. As they'd done for forty years, they dressed for bed separately, in the bathroom, Maria first. When she came out in her flannel nightgown, he went in. Then he got into bed beside her and curled around her back. He put his left arm over her. She took his hand. "Good night," she said.

"Good night."

She was the sleeper, he the thinker. He thought back over the day. Her breathing deepened as she took leave of the world. Her hand twitched; her leg jumped—she was already dreaming.

He thought about the universe, the great golden machine, the infinity of parts in perfect fit. Inside it there, between tick and tock, were Maria, Massimo, and himself. The thing moved soundlessly, slowly awhirl, and God's eyes, never sleeping, watched.

Idiots

Dick and Jane Sonnenschein came to Florence for adventure. They had both had adventures before they married, but not nearly enough marital adventures. They brought their daughter, Debbie, along, of course. In fact, it was because of Debbie that they chose Florence. She was ten years old, and they wanted her to learn Dante's language, Tuscan, the purest Italian. Neither of the parents spoke Italian and they regretted it. Since they were too old now to master it fully, they at least wanted their daughter to have the chance.

When they arrived in Florence, they stayed at a pensione while looking for an apartment. Without the language, they realized, it would be hopeless trying to find a place through the newspapers, so Dick went to the Florentine campus of his university and inquired. His university was represented, in a single room on the fourth floor of a house in Piazza del Limbo, by a middle-aged woman with a dark mustache who understood very little English.

She wrote out the name of an agency near Porta Romana—a good long walk from the pensione. But walk they did, the three of them, following their map along the traffic-choked, narrow streets, and marveling at the ancient stone buildings along the way. Maukpauktauk, Connecticut, was old, but nothing like this. Here the stones reeked of age, of history. Undoubtedly, blood had run in these streets, and the thought that Michelangelo, Leonardo, and Dante might have taken this same route thrilled them no end. They both loved history.

Debbie, though, got tired before they reached the agency, and while they were talking to the agent, a solemn man who fortunately spoke English, she interrupted to say she wanted to go home. She meant home to Maukpauktauk. Jane comforted her, as Dick jotted down two addresses. Debbie said, "I have to poop." Jane tested her phrase-book Italian by asking, *"Dov'è il gabinetto?"* The agent winced. "Down the hall, second door to the right."

They liked the first place they saw. The landlady showed them two large bedrooms, a study, a living room, a kitchen and bath. Outside one of the bedrooms and the study ran a little *terrazzina,* a balcony, and Dick could just see himself sitting at his typewriter out there, banging away. He had come to Florence to write. Dante had written there, and he admired Dante. He'd brought his portable typewriter and lots of paper.

Jane had come for background. She wanted the Medici, the Art, the History of the place. There were literally centuries of background here—you couldn't go anywhere in the city without walking through background. Why, religion alone—all those huge churches—would take weeks to master.

Jane asked the landlady about a school for Debbie. The landlady stared. Jane plunged into her phrase book. *"Dov'è la scuola per la bambina?"* The landlady wore a black, unadorned, widow's dress. She frowned and shrugged. But when Jane pointed at Debbie and read a book in pantomime, the light dawned in her face, and a string of language exploded like firecrackers on her tongue.

With her hands, she indicated a series of directions, this way and that.

"Beany—good," Dick said. Jane corrected him: "Baynie."

They agreed on the rent—450,000 lire per month—and a deposit of two months' rent against damages. It was more than they could afford, but they'd yearned for this trip. It was worth it just to be here, though it would take, over and beyond Dick's small half-pay from his university, everything they'd saved. Even then they would have to cut corners, but think of it, a whole academic year in Florence using every moment to expand their minds! With such freedom, who knew how far they might go, what they might accomplish?

They had already cashed lots of traveler's checks at the train station. They counted out an astonishing pile of lire onto the living-room table. They received a receipt, signed, "Dottore Inelda Antonini." Dick said, "I'm a doctor, too—a doctor of philosophy, of literature." He pointed his thumb at his forehead. The landlady opened her purse and, beaming, gave him a packet of aspirin.

Although they'd gotten an apartment on the first try, they wouldn't congratulate themselves until Debbie had an assigned place in school. They went down the six flights of stairs to the street, then followed the landlady's directions as well as they could. They got lost for a while, and argued, but they came eventually to the Scuola Speciale Giuseppe Verdi.

They found the office just off the courtyard. At a large desk sat a middle-aged woman with her glasses hanging from strings around her neck. This was Jane's job. Flipping the pages of her phrase book, she managed to ask if Debbie could enter the school. Debbie stood between Dick and Jane, staring obstinately at her shoes. The principal asked how old she was. Jane said, "Fifth grade, but maybe lower because of the language. She's smart—*intelligente.* She'll learn fast—*subito.*"

The principal looked with compassion from one parent to the other, then said, "I understand. Yes, there is room. Bring her tomorrow morning. School is six days a week, from nine o'clock until twelve-thirty."

Jane struggled with the words, then found one of her own. "Books?"

"We have everything. The state provides."

She gave Jane a form to fill out. It took a while, even leaving some of the lines empty. When she'd done all she could, she gave it over. The principal read it and said, *"Sonnenschein, ja. Il sole."* She pointed upward and made a round face in the air.

Then she came from behind the desk, gently lifted Debbie's chin, and said, "Deborah, *un'ebrea piccola. Bella, bellissima."* She stroked Debbie's hair.

Dick and Jane were pleased no end. In a strange city, a foreign city, to be settled the first day—the gods must be with them! First, of course, they had to move the luggage. There was lots of it: two large suitcases apiece, plus shoulder bags and Dick's typewriter. They treated themselves to a taxi.

But the cab couldn't levitate. They had to haul all that weight up six flights. They finished, panting. Dick said, "Jesus and Mary, what a climb." Debbie had chosen her room and began unpacking her toys. Dick and Jane didn't unpack. It had been a hard day. They stretched out on the bed, first removing their shoes because of the large deposit against damages, and soon their hands found each other's. Jane said, "Here we are, in Florence." Dick said, "By God, we did it."

They felt too weak to shop, then cook, so they went out for their last big splurge before submitting to their budget. It was a wonderful dinner. They'd never tasted such pasta, the chicken was done beautifully, and the vegetables, though overcooked, certainly tasted nourishing. The wine overwhelmed them. A classic Chianti six years old, it cost only four dollars, and how it brought out the full flavor of the food!

Tired, a little drunk, and tremendously excited, they finally did congratulate themselves. With small glasses of brandy, they made a toast, "To a wonderful year." Debbie joined the toast with her glass of mineral water.

That evening at about nine o'clock, when Debbie was sound asleep and Jane was having a bath, Dick, in his pajamas, heard someone fumbling at the door lock. He stepped into the hallway as the door opened. Dottore Antonini entered. Behind her, all but hidden by her bulk, came a small, stooped, grinning man of sixty-five or so. The signora said, *"Scusi, eh? Questo è mio marito."* She indicated the little man. Her husband? He put both fists on his chest and said, *"Soldati Luigi, io. Non si disturbi*—not disturb." The two of them disappeared into the study and shut the door.

Dick waited in the bed. After her bath, Jane came in, took off her robe, and got into bed beside him. "I feel great," she said, "tired but, well, just right." He snapped the switch on the bed lamp. She kissed his ear, then threw a leg over him.

"We'd better not," he said.

"No? Tired? Well . . ."

"There's someone here," he said.

"Here? Where?"

"In there—in the study. It's Mrs. Antonini and, I think, her husband, I think his name is Luigi."

"They're sleeping here? On the floor?"

"I don't think so. I heard a thump. There must be a pull-down bed in there."

"Strange," she said.

It was still strange when, the next morning at six, Dick got up to start writing his first short story. His typewriter and paper were out of reach in the study. Since they hadn't bought groceries, there wasn't any coffee to lighten his mood, so he sat stolidly at the kitchen table and waited.

At seven Luigi shuffled in in his slippers and a polka-dot flannel nightshirt. *"Scusi, eh?"* he said. He put water in the espresso pot, filled the net with coffee from a package he'd brought in with him, screwed the top on, and set it on the stove. He glanced sideways at Dick, then said slily, "Il Duce." Arms folded, Dick watched him.

When the coffee was done, he took the pot and two cups into the other room. Dick sat there. Twenty minutes later, Dottore Antonini sailed out like a black pirate ship, towing Luigi in her wake. *"Buon giorno, scusi,"* she said. She waited while Luigi cleaned the coffeepot, said, *"Scusi,"* again, and they left.

Dick stuck his head into the study and sniffed. Yes, two mature people, who didn't bathe often, had slept there. What looked like a long cabinet in the wall was a fold-out bed.

He awakened Jane and Debbie. They all rushed around, getting dressed. Outside, the only place they could find for breakfast was a bar. Dick and Jane had cappuccino and a sweet roll, Debbie a glass of milk, a roll, and a pear. At the school, they turned their daughter over to the principal, then left to start their day.

"What does *scusi* mean?" he said.

"Pardon—excuse me."

"Well, I've been scusied enough. I wonder when they'll leave."

"Oh, don't worry about it—it's a transition. Let's not let it spoil things. I'm off to the Uffizi—I've heard so much about it. Will you retrieve Debbie at twelve-thirty? Stop and buy some lunch things? In case I get caught up?"

"Sure—yep. *Scusi, eh?*"

At the apartment, he threw open the study window to air the place out, then set up his typewriter, rolled in a sheet of paper, and sat there. There were hundreds of stories he could tell, things that had happened to him, lots of interesting incidents. Which one should he begin with?

Eleven o'clock came and went, and then it was noon. To be on the safe side, he took his writing things into the bedroom, then left for the school. With Debbie in hand, he could shop.

The courtyard now was full of parents, chatting in small groups, and at the bell they all turned toward the door. Children poured out, skipping and stumbling, the teachers holding some of them by the hand, others rolling on their own toward their parents. Debbie appeared, in the steady grip of a wiry woman with gray hair, who, when she'd transferred Debbie's hand to his, said, *"Una bambina tranquilla. Buon giorno, signore."*

On the way home, Debbie was quiet. He said, "What did you do this morning?"

"Colored. We cut out some things. Some of the kids couldn't."

"Did you read?"

"She let me read a book. It was an alphabet book. She helped me pronounce the letters and some words."

"Good," he said. "It's a good start. We'll have you speaking Italian in no time."

"Dad?"

"Yes, sweetie?"

"There's something wrong with those kids. They're really weird."

"Well, it's a foreign school, sweetie. It's bound to be strange at first. You'll get used to it."

They were already at the apartment when Dick remembered lunch. "Oh oh, let's go shopping," he said. They went back down the stairs. But in the street, they found all the stores closed. "What the hell?" he said. They walked all of the nearby streets, and finally, in a bar again, settled for squares of pizza, with milk for Debbie and a beer for himself.

They trudged up the stairs again. Inside, he said, "Daddy's going to have a little nap, sweetie. You play—all right?"

Jane woke him up at four. "The cupboard is bare. What happened?"

"The stores were closed."

"They always close in the afternoon. You were supposed to go before they closed."

"I was writing," he said. "I can't just drop everything and run out shopping."

"Never mind, I'll do it," she said, and slammed out.

In an hour and a half, she returned, still smoldering, loaded down with plastic bags full of things. "Now that I've shopped, I'll cook," she said.

He heard her banging around in the kitchen.

Dinner, though, came out just fine—Southern fried chicken, baked potatoes, and string beans with lemon butter. After a bottle of wine, they felt much better. He apologized for his lapse that morning, she for losing her temper. They resolved to make a new start and proceed reasonably. Tomorrow it would be her turn to leave Debbie at school and pick her up, his turn to cook dinner. They would split the chores down the middle, decorously, fairly, rationally.

"What did you see at the Uffizi?" he said.

"Masterpieces. Nothing but masterpieces. My God, there are so many—I'll have to go back again."

While he did the dishes, she spent some time with Debbie and then, to get an early start on tomorrow, they went to bed. This time they did make love, and were just drifting toward sleep when they heard the key in the lock. Then they heard the large sounds that people make when they try moving softly.

The next morning, Dick, at the kitchen table, was staring at his typewriter when Luigi came in. *"Scusi, eh?"* he said, and put the coffee on. While waiting, he looked at Dick's typewriter and said, *"Macchina da scrivere*—teep-wreeter. Ha." He pointed to the stove. *"Caffettiera*—cohfee poht. Eengleesh, eh?"

He took the coffee into the study. When the pair emerged, and while Luigi washed the dishes, Dottore Antonini spoke rapidly, pointing at the typewriter, clasping her hands under her chin, extending her arms wide. Then they left.

After Jane and Debbie departed for school, sweet calm descended. He still hadn't written anything, but at least he could begin thinking of what to write. He thought all morning, and then, at noon, began a letter to the chairman of his department back in Connecticut, letting him know that they'd arrived in Florence.

Jane burst in, dragging Debbie. "You fool—you didn't even notice," she said. "Are you totally stupid? That's a school for the retarded. Debbie's going to class with a bunch of idiots!"

"She is?"

"Of course she is. How could you miss it?"

"It's all right," Debbie said. "They're nice—I like it."

"We'll have you out of there," Jane said, "tomorrow. God, Dick."

"The teacher's nice," Debbie said. "She talks real slow. I can understand her."

Jane slapped sandwiches together. As they ate, Dick said, "I don't know, it might not be a bad idea to leave her there. She's happy."

"With idiots? You're out of your mind."

"She teaches me to talk," Debbie said. "She shows me where to put my tongue. *Buon giorno. Come sta? Vuoi un bicchiere di latte?* That means do you want a glass of milk."

"Beautiful," Dick said. "Hear that, Jane? Maybe they give individual attention—take the kids from wherever they are and see how far they can go."

In spite of herself, Jane was impressed. She looked thoughtfully at Debbie. "But what about the socializing? What kind of exchange can she have with a bunch of retards?"

"Massimo's not a retard. He's nice. I help him with the cutouts and he talks to me."

"See?" Dick said. "Anyway, haven't we always been against homogeneity? Isn't that why we sent her to the Lincoln school back home?"

They decided to try it for another week.

Today Jane took a nap. She'd spent the morning at the Palazzo Vecchio and was wiped out. Dick finished his letter to the chairman, then walked to the central post office to learn how to mail it.

On the way back, he stopped at the *rosticceria* and bought a sack-ful of croquettes, three spinach balls, and some roasted potatoes.

Later, as he was heating these things, Jane came to the kitchen and slumped in a chair at the table. "She thinks we're Jews. That principal—remember, she called Debbie *un'ebrea bellissima?* I looked it up. It means beautiful Jewess. God almighty, it's depressing."

"We don't look Jewish," Dick said. "It's our name, I guess. Anything that ends with 'schein.' But what's the difference? We have nothing against Jews."

"But to be called one . . ."

"Think how they feel, then. They're called Jews all the time."

"That's different—they are Jews."

"Well, we don't care, do we? It's not what we're called, it's what we are that's important. Let them call us anything they like. We know what we are."

"I guess you're right," she said. "You are right—we don't care. But even so—"

"Dinner's ready. Let's eat."

* * *

In time they grew accustomed to the routine of life in Florence. They began to like the afternoon siesta, when everything shut down for three hours. They learned how to shop, where to buy stationery and stamps, and what the signs meant in the shop windows. Painfully, with a dictionary, they learned to read the newspaper, but when it came to speaking, Debbie was the star. She learned by leaps, and they agreed that the special school was a good thing after all. Jane saw so many Crucifixions, Descents from the Cross, Mothers and Childs with Saints, and Christs Ascendent that her head swam. She shifted from painting to sculpture. Dick still hadn't found a story to write, though he put in his hours at the typewriter, writing letters to all his friends and to a lot of people he didn't much care for, and began keeping a journal.

The one thing they didn't get used to was the Dottore and her little husband, who still crept in at night and vanished in the morning. What did they do all day; where did they go? Why, if they were married, didn't they have the same last name? "Dottore," they learned, covered a wide range of possibilities, including those implied by "doctor" in America. But here even used-car salesmen were called dottore. Ostensibly, the word meant "a laureate, a graduate from a university," but apparently anyone, graduate or not, could assume that title for himself.

Dick learned a few things about Luigi, who was proud of his English and liked a little conversation while his morning coffee was cooking. He was sixty-four years old, a veteran of World War II, and a great admirer of Benito Mussolini. He had fought against the Americans at Monte Cassino. He'd been a lieutenant. The Americans were brave, but not as brave as the Italians. Next to the Italians, he admired the Germans. One morning he opened his wallet and displayed, in facing plastic envelopes, pictures of Il Duce and Adolf Hitler saluting each other.

Once in a while, from the late-night, muffled, scuffling noises in the study, Dick and Jane deduced that the war was continuing. Once in a while, there was a slap followed by a squeak. "Poor Luigi," Dick said. Jane said, "They've got to go."

"There might be some trouble about that. We don't have a contract."

"If you were so stupid as not to get a contract—"

"We," he corrected her. "Anyway, language is your province, yours and that phrase book's."

"It's past Thanksgiving, and they're still here."

"They don't celebrate Thanksgiving in Italy."

"Go talk to that agent, what's his name—Pifferini."

Dick went. He explained the situation; asked what could be done. The agent sighed and said, "What you speak of is very

common in Italy. There's a rent-control ordinance, strictly en-
forced, by which if a renter sublets his apartment he loses his
privilege."

"What privilege?"

"The privilege of paying a very low rent."

"How low? How much do they pay, would you guess?"

"Oh, not more than 80,000, maybe less."

"And we're paying 450,000? And they're living with us? Why
didn't you warn us?"

The agent sighed again. "My function is to bring together those
who have and those who need."

"But this is outrageous. I can't use my own study. How do I get
rid of them?"

"Mr. Sonnenschein, please, where would they go? They have no
other place."

"I don't care where they go—I want them out."

The agent looked away, then back. "In Florence," he said,
"things fit." He interlaced his fingers to demonstrate. "Now when
something doesn't fit, it's a question of which piece is wrong. Do
you see what I mean?"

"But they rented us the apartment."

"Of course they did."

"And they won't move out."

"Probably not."

"So, what can we do? It isn't fair."

"Move out yourselves."

"Good—we'll do it. What vacancies do you have listed?"

"At the moment, none. You were lucky. Because of the ordinance, there are very few vacancies in Florence. My advice to you,
signore, is to accommodate yourself to the situation." He showed
Dick his compactly interlaced fingers.

When Dick explained this to Jane, she said, "They're screwing
us right and left, upside down and downside up. God, what a

country. It's a conspiracy to rob rich foreigners. We're not rich, we're just scraping by."

"But we came all the way from America. Neither of us works, and we pay 450,000 lire a month. Try convincing anyone that we're not rich."

"My shoes are worn out from walking. I can't afford new ones. And those goddamned stairs. Haven't these people heard about elevators?"

"I know, I know."

"Don't patronize me, you prick. Just get rid of those schnorrers in the other room."

At that point, a thing happened that he wouldn't have believed. He smacked her hard across the mouth. Shocked, he looked at his hand. She said nothing. She stared at him, and he'd never seen such hatred in anyone's face—pure rock, as in the aeons before there was life on earth.

* * *

Christmas came and went, with extravagant displays of gifts in the stores. They bought what they could for Debbie but only very small things for each other. It seemed that prices went up every time they turned around, and the exchange rate fell by two hundred lire per dollar, which took 15 percent from their buying power. Every time they went to American Express, the news was worse. On January 6, they learned, the children got another round of presents—it was Epiphany, a big holiday in Italy. So they bought Debbie more things. It turned very cold and began snowing, so without doubt Jane and Debbie would have to have winter coats.

They began eating meat only every third day. They bought ordinary wine and limited themselves to one glass apiece, at dinner. Dick stopped writing letters, to save the postage money, and didn't start writing stories. For some reason, he couldn't find the rhythm, the tone, the voice. He began wondering if he had any intelligence at all. When Jane stopped going to churches and museums and just hung around the apartment, day after day, he got fed up. "Go," he said, "leave me alone. You're like a dark cloud, like a cholera epidemic."

"I want a divorce," she said.

"A divorce—shit, in Italy?"

"Either those people go, or I go. Make up your mind."

"I've already made it up," he said.

They glared at each other.

In February the Dottore and Luigi got sick. They didn't leave the house. Every so often, the study door would open and one of them, bathrobe flapping, would dash to the toilet. Dick and Jane heard the wheezing, coughing, groaning in there, and occasionally the sound of raised voices. Jane said, "They're poisoning us. They stink. Stick your nose in the bathroom."

"All right, let's go back to America," he said. "We might as well admit it, this hasn't worked out. Let's cut our losses."

"Our plane reservation isn't till June. There's a big penalty if we change it. Anyway, go back where in America? We rented our house, remember? With a contract?"

He looked out at the heavy sky, at the snowflakes drifting. "What kind of people are we? Is this what we're like? We're worthless, we're total failures. Take away our car, our house, our supermarkets, we fall apart. I've never been so goddamn miserable in my life. We're not even decent human beings. A decent human being would take those people in there some soup."

But just then there was a spate of squabbling in the study. They heard a shriek, slaps, a yelp, and heavy puffing. The door flew open, Luigi flew out, and bits of paper fluttered all around. *"I miei documenti!"* he said.

"Fuck your documents," Jane said, kicking at the bits of paper. Like a stegosaurus, the signora filled the doorway. She grabbed Jane's hair and shook her, while Dick tried getting between them.

Luigi pummeled his back with small sharp fists. Dick turned and pushed his face gently but firmly.

When they fell away from one another, Dick said, "Okay, that's it—out! Out, you two—*via! Fuori!* Get the hell out!" He pointed at the door.

The Dottore raised herself a few inches and said, *"Pneu, pneu!"*

Dick said, "Now, *ora, adesso!"* and showed his fist. Jane meanwhile had gone into the study. She emerged with an armful of clothing, took it to the front door, and chucked it down the stairs.

Luigi tore his hair. *"Aou,* signora, signore," he said. Jane was pulling sheets and blankets from the bed. She flung them out onto the landing.

The Dottore deflated as if someone had pulled her stopper. She went into the study and began putting things in a satchel. Luigi found a suitcase at the back of a closet. Dick and Jane watched as they removed food, papers, toilet articles, and clothing from various drawers in the room. The last thing they took was the coffeepot.

"Don't come back till June," Dick said. *"Fino a giugno."*

"Pneu," said the Dottore.

When the door was shut, they heard them outside, scrambling around, picking things up—already arguing. The doorbell rang. Dick called out, "Not till June!"

The Dottore huffed. *"Ignoramo!"*

Jane opened the study windows to air the place out. Dick brought his typewriter in and set up shop on the desk. Jane swept the bits of paper into a pile. Dick held the dustpan for her.

They looked at each other. She said, "My God, what a brawl."

They burst out laughing.

Easter was lovely, warm and sunny, and great crowds of people, dressed in their best, strolled along the Arno. Dick and Jane and Debbie walked and walked. Near the Trinity Bridge, Debbie said, "Hey, there's Massimo!" She ran over to a boy who dipped and slid along between his parents. When Massimo saw her, he rolled his head and began jabbering. The parents glanced around, saw Dick and Jane, and smiled.

"*Sono amici, eh?*" Dick said. "They're friends. Dick Sonnen-schein. This is Jane."

They all shook hands. Debbie and Massimo were both jabbering now, understanding each other perfectly, though Massimo took time out to howl, and then Debbie got into a rapid-fire conversation with the parents.

"Can I go to Massimo's house?" she said. "They invited me."

"You bet you can," said Jane. "Just find out where it is, so we'll know."

Debbie did, then said, "It's all right, they'll bring me home at seven."

So Massimo took Debbie's hand and lurched along beside her, his parents following. Dick and Jane watched. They couldn't have been happier.

In fact, they were very happy generally these days. Dick had given up the notion of writing—he'd decided he wasn't meant to be a writer—and had plunged into the museums, finding lots of material he could use in his courses. After all, the Italian Renaissance was the fertile soil in which the English Renaissance sprouted some years later. Jane took over the typewriter to do some impressions of Florence for the Maukpauktauk *News,* to which she'd formerly contributed several articles on gardening. Here she concentrated on the gardens of Florence, particularly the Boboli Gardens, behind the Pitti Palace. Dick thought her work very insightful, a good cut above anything else she'd written for the paper.

They saw the Dottore but once a month, when she came for the rent. But exorbitant as the rent was, it was only money, and they paid it gladly, gladly did without lots of things, for the privilege of living in this wonderful city. There was the matter of the deposit, of course, which sometimes cast a shadow. It was money they could ill afford to leave in Italy, and they sensed that getting it back from the Dottore would be about as easy as drawing her through the keyhole.

They didn't worry overmuch, however. They still had April, May, and June to think about it. For the moment, life was pretty good—in fact, great—and they filled every moment of it.

* * *

They cleaned the house thoroughly. It took them two whole days to do the kind of job they could be proud of. And all the time they were packing as well. They had made a reservation at a pensione, in case there should be some trouble at the last—in case, say, the Dottore should catch flu. To penetrate the language barrier, they'd asked Mr. Pifferini to be present.

What a rush that last hour was as they packed their things, put the final touches on the apartment. But they were ready, their bags piled by the door, when the Dottore and Luigi arrived. They stood uncomfortably for a few minutes, but then the agent came. Dick escorted the party through the apartment, showing each gleaming room. Luigi grinned and gave esctatic little bursts of laughter. Obviously he'd never seen the place so shiny. But the Dottore frowned.

She did the inventory. There had been some breakage, but not much, and besides, the Sonnenscheins had added a few things, such as a new coffeepot. So they were feeling pretty confident when they all sat down at the table in the living room.

For the breakage, the Dottore demanded huge reparations. Dick offered next to nothing. They compromised somewhere near the middle. Then there was the gas. Jane pointed out that the proprietors themselves had used gas when they lived with their tenants. As each of these items was settled, Luigi pressed the buttons of his pocket calculator.

Central heating was a major expense. Electricity, water, and garbage, too. Dick reminded them that the garbage service was free, provided by the city. "Hot water!" said the Dottore. Dick guessed that the building was heated by a boiler, in which case it would cost nothing to heat the water.

The agent didn't say much. At the end, when Luigi totaled it all up, the Dottore laid four 100,000-lire bills on the table. It was a bit less than half the deposit. The agent reached out and lifted up one of the bills. "For my time," he said.

Their dismay was brief. They really couldn't complain. They shifted their luggage from inside to outside, and Dick went downstairs and out to a pay phone, to call a cab.

They spent their last night in Florence, as they'd spent their first, at a pensione near the train station. The next day they took the train to Zurich. On the day after that, they flew to New York City, and from there they took the train to Maukpauktauk, Connecticut.

Leaning Man

He awoke against his wall in the train station, bent double. His hands hung to the tops of his gray canvas shoes. He had been dreaming of the clock on the tower of the Palazzo Vecchio, and now, as if the dream hadn't quite ended, he saw circles on the green marble floor. Coins! People had been good to him again. Look there, while he slept, someone had tucked a one-thousand-lira note between his bare ankle and the top of his shoe!

From a dream of time, one doesn't leap straight into action. Moving only his eyes, he saw a line of feet at the currency exchange—foreigners, trading strange money for good Italian lire. Crossing that line, through the gaps, went streams of shoes, to and from the trains. Shoes everywhere, black, brown, blue—sports shoes, sandals, high heels and low, and boots in all styles, conditions, and colors. What a variety of footwear! What a variety of things in the world!

To pick up the coins, all he had to do was bend a bit more. Bending was easy. There, he had twenty-three hundred lire, more than twice what he would need for the day. But when he moved, someone noticed, and a voice said, "Good morning, Tozzo—may I bring you coffee?"

Ah, the run-over heels, the two baggage trucks—Aurelio always pushed one truck and pulled another. Twice the bags, twice the tips. Tozzo shook his head—too early for coffee. Let a man get awake first.

He began by putting his hands on his thighs, not to support his weight but to get the circulation going. He had big hands for one his size—a stoneworker's hands. Spread out, they covered his pants from pockets to knees. He squeezed and relaxed his fists, and like twin hearts they set the blood flowing. To bring feeling to his shoulders, he moved his elbows back and forth. He rotated his head to loosen the neck.

Now he was ready to say hello to his oldest friend, the pain. It kept house some five inches above his waist, where the spine angled. As he straightened, it woke up and said, "Let's spend all day together." He straightened to the limit, ninety degrees, and groaned. He could get hired as a carpenter's square.

But what was that lump between him and the wall? He reached behind and pulled it out—a pack of cigarettes. What was he, a bucket, a catchall? People tossed things his way all night. Whenever he awakened, he found surprises. Of course, people wanted something in return—good health, good luck, the past erased, a bright future. They were human, after all. They had wants and worries.

He smoked facedown. The smoke stung his eyes and used his nose for a chimney, but it cleared the dust from his head. Now where was Aurelio? With coffee on top of the cigarette, he could fly out over Florence, have a look at the Arno, at that clock he'd dreamed of, at the Duomo, in the center of town. He would love seeing the Duomo again, the green-, white-, and rose-colored marble, the great size of it, bulking up over the city. If he could move as well as he could think, wouldn't he swoop around?

He pushed off the wall and started for the rest room, but within a few steps a voice stopped him. "Breakfast, Tozzo?" Black boots, blue pants, a sweet roll on a napkin. This was the Capo, controller of all baggage, an important man. Tozzo shook his head and the roll went away, but not before he felt a light touch on his back. Even the Capo wanted something.

In the echoing, U-shaped station, he lived at bottom-center, in the room where people bought tickets, newspapers, and Italian money. His bathroom was a long way off, on the left side of the U, past the seventeen sets of train tracks that branched to all parts of the world. As he went through the crowd, the loudspeaker announced trains arriving, trains departing; and people who knew him, porters, brakemen, engineers, and conductors—and the men who sold food and drink on the platforms—all of these made a point of speaking to him, offering something, touching him.

At the rest room, where others had to pay, the man in charge let him in for nothing, and even gave him a towel and soap. Tozzo used the toilet, then washed his face and neck and the top of his head. By the feel of his beard, it was Saturday. Hair was as good as a calendar. If his head hadn't gone bald, he could have told the months.

Saturday? Good. He would travel today, visit his barber in Via de' Fossi, give the old legs a workout. In the old days, he could have dashed that far in less than five minutes, but now, unless he wanted to spend the night outside, he had better start off.

He went as he'd come, but as he passed the tracks on the way to the exit, a certain pair of brown strap boots stepped in front of him. Green pants, the skirt of the tan raincoat—trouble! "Santo Tozzo, please!" said the voice. Tozzo was too slow to get around him, and there came the hand, with paper money between the fingers, weaving like a snake, striking at his collar, shirt pocket, belt.

He dodged the money, but then the man fell to his knees before him and looked up. He had a black, nose-wide mustache, yellowish eyes, and cheeks full of blood. It was a face that made Tozzo glad he didn't have to see many faces anymore. "Bless me, Tozzo —have mercy on my soul!"

"Go to a priest," Tozzo said. He moved, but the man crawled in front of him and grabbed his feet. A crowd formed as the man babbled. Tozzo clapped his hands over his ears and said, "I'm no saint, go to the police!" But the misshapen mouth continued straining. It had bubbles of spit in the corners. Tozzo shut his eyes.

How long did it last? When he chanced a look, the man had vanished, the crowd had dispersed, and he was no longer at the center of anything. The man, so crazy that he made Tozzo feel crazy, caught him like this every few days, having gotten it into his head that Tozzo had powers. He had no powers. He had a bent back, he spent his life standing, and that was all.

Leaving the station, he came to the first dangerous crossing. But the cars kindly stopped or swerved, and he made it to the other side. From a newsstand, someone called, "Hey, Tozzo," but he didn't stop. He had his feet in rhythm now, and he kept going. Now for the second street. Horns and brakes! A friendly motorcycle curved in and accompanied him to the curb, and then the rider touched his shoulder.

If people thought he brought them luck, that was their business —he couldn't make their thoughts for them. But he had no powers. A power was something that reached out and did things. A power could work magic, make life better, cure a sickness in the body or mind. He couldn't do things like that. His gift, if he had one, was passive.

Memory, that's what he had. Why, he remembered working on the walls of the Duomo when Florence was hardly more than a town. A craftsman with hammer and chisel, with a craftsman's eye for the grain of the marble, he had stood on the high wall as the great blocks were hoisted up and had fitted them so that even air couldn't find the seams. After all these centuries, weren't there still dried stains between the blocks, the salty remnants of sweat that dropped from his chin, back when he was straight and strong?

He'd once told a friend, a leather worker named Sergio, about this gift of his. Friend though he was, Sergio had laughed. "That's impossible, Tozzo. This is the twentieth century. Are you immortal?"

Tozzo didn't know if he was or not. He said, "Do you remember being born?" Sergio said, "Are you crazy? No one does."

But Tozzo did. He remembered standing by a river in a crowd of small souls, waiting to be carried over into the world. He remembered his mother's heartbeat, and her muscles gripping as she pushed him out. He remembered being left at the Bigallo, where people took in stray infants, and taking hold of a nun's big finger. She said, "What a tiny bite he is, but feel how strong."

Since everyone needed a name, the nuns gave him his: Tozzo Pioppo. Tozzo for morsel, Pioppo for poplar. Saint Morsel, Saint Little Bit—it made him laugh to think of it. If he was a tree, he'd become a bent one.

He couldn't say just when he'd begun bending, for time was like the light around him, now close as a coat, now wide as the sky. But he remembered a doctor examining his spine, and the words "degenerative, irreversible, probably hereditary." He remembered the body brace.

The brace was painful—he couldn't work while wearing it. He got so he couldn't work without it, either. Sergio, a master craftsman, fashioned a padded leather collar for his neck, with a strap that went down his back, came through and split around his sex, then hooked to his belt in two places in front. It gave some relief.

But pain can be either friend or enemy. If you defend against it, you'll have to fight for your life. Make it your friend, and go free. What a blessed day it was when he removed the collar. He stopped lying down to sleep, stopped sitting, and no longer needed his room behind the barbershop. He moved to the railroad station and took up residence against the wall, he and the pain. Around his neck and down his back, coming between his legs and tied to his belt, he still wore a piece of string. It gave no support. He wore it in memory of Sergio, who had died a long time ago.

The bells of Santa Maria Novella—noon already! But he hadn't been standing still, he'd made good time, and here were the paving stones of the piazza, worn and speckled with pigeon droppings. A hand took his elbow and he saw a black skirt and black, square-toed shoes. She accompanied him a short way, then released him, saying, "Be well, Santo Tozzo." If a nun calls you a saint, you'd better act like one. He blessed all the pigeons in the piazza.

Like his father and grandfather, the barber was named Michael, and for pure genius he could have descended from Michelangelo himself. He helped Tozzo onto a stool and worked underneath him: first, hot towels, then thick lather, then the razor. Back and forth he moved, the blade flashing, touching always firmly and with the same pressure. Then, after another hot towel, came a liquid so cold and astringent that it numbed Tozzo's skin. He felt the way *David* must have felt when Michelangelo finished, so smooth and cool—a face for the centuries!

Helping him down, the barber said, "I see you're rich." He plucked a ten-thousand-lira note from Tozzo's belt. Ah, the sick man in the strap boots—the snake had struck after all.

"Take it," he said. "You're paid, for once."

"Do you want me to die from shock?" He stuffed the bill into Tozzo's collar.

Well, if no one wanted the money, maybe the pigeons could use it. In the piazza, he found the strolling seed man and spent it all. When he scattered the grain, what a roar of wings, what a gabble of bird tongues! There couldn't be that many pigeons in the world!

He got away without stepping on any toes. But all the excitement had tired him out. He shuffled to the church for a rest. Leaning against the facade in the warm sun, listening to the pigeons, he thought he might as well treat himself to a *pisolino,* a short nap.

The bells again, booming in the air, vibrating through the stone against his back. He saw his shoes, his hands hanging, and more coins. He picked them up. As he was straightening, a priest stopped to help. "Thank you, Father, here," he said, and pressed the coins into the soft hand.

The nap didn't refresh him as it should have done. He was still tired, more than before, and with all those streets to cross. He was thirsty, too. He hadn't had a drink all day. At the first bar he came to, he stopped and asked for water. The waiter offered wine and sweet cakes as well, but he took only the water. The waiter touched his back.

He arrived home as the loudspeaker was announcing the express from Rome. That meant 8:06, dinnertime. He went to the self-serve restaurant, where others were waiting in line. Not Tozzo. No, the moment he appeared, a bowl of thick minestrone floated in beneath his nose. It was a fragrance worth living for—nothing in the world smelled so good. He held up his one-thousand-lira note, but no one took it. He stepped to one side, ate the soup, and saw the bowl and spoon float away.

Could he be tired again already? It seemed he'd just finished a nap. "Well, I'm slowing down," he said. Belly full, a rich man in spite of himself, he went to his bedroom and leaned on the wall. The currency exchange had closed, the newsstand showed steel shutters, and the traffic to and from the trains had thinned. It was as if, in the huge enclosure, the air itself were settling for sleep.

He smoked another cigarette. He shut his eyes.

Time was like a pear, pear-shaped, golden, flecked with brown. At the beginning, it had opened out swiftly, then rounded to fullness, then begun narrowing. He saw the pear fallen and wasps humming lazily around. He saw autumn light like gold on the fallen fruit, on the green grass, on the moving wasps.

Someone touched him. A coin rang on the marble. The golden wasps sang in the light.

First Love

We came into this money, I mean my dad did, when an uncle of his back in Illinois died. It was enough to buy a car in the BMW price range, or to expand the kitchen. He likes to cook. He wouldn't mind driving a fine car, either. When he got the check in the mail, he squinted one eye and opened the other really wide, then said, "Stephanie, we'd better think this over."

His face moves a lot. When he thinks, he gets his eyebrows into it. If he feels good, he oversmiles, and when he laughs, it's like an earthquake in Calabria—everything shakes. I think that's one of the reasons why my mother divorced him and went to Cleveland. It would be reason enough. He feels too good too often, without any cause that I can see. Living with someone like that, day in, day out, wears you down. When he walks, he sort of bounces, he snaps his fingers in time, and if you're with him you want to cross the street and look at a window display of surgical instruments.

"This is a once-in-a-lifetime thing, kid," he said. "We could invest it for our old age. We could blow it in Acapulco or Las Vegas, have fun, bust some bubbles. On the other hand, we could send you to college back East, buy you a primo education. What do you think?"

He uses questions the way bankers smile—to make you think it's a partnership. He picked up the habit from teaching. He teaches American history at a community college in Sunnyvale, where I've seen him in action a couple of times. "If you were Ben Franklin, what would you say to General Lafayette at this point?" Ain't this cheese a little old? Where do you keep the bimbos, General? It's a required course for students wanting to transfer to a real college with real professors. They sit there like mushrooms. He asked the question, he can answer it.

Try irony on him and see how far you get. "I think we ought to corner the gold market," I said.

"Good point," he said. "You're absolutely right. The trick is to parlay this found money into a future for us both, in a way that will bring pleasure and a payoff. Pleasure is essential, as I see it. I'm no puritan—I don't believe in mortification of the flesh for the good of the spirit."

That's another reason why Mother divorced him. He spread his flesh around Sunnyvale, and word got back. He pleaded no contest. She took her share of the property settlement to her second husband, Eddie, back in Cleveland Heights. I spend the summers with them and work at Eddie's Cleaners. It's depressing. For one thing, if your name is Edie you should never marry a man named Eddie, no matter how glittering his business acumen. On the other hand, you probably should divorce Bob—either that or run in front of a truck on I-280.

"I mean," he said, "why shouldn't we invest this money in a living trust—in ourselves? Who else can we trust, eh? If life had worked out differently, I would be Professor of Renaissance History at Harvard or Oxford by now. I love the Renaissance, always have. American history's a rivulet—I long for thundering rivers, the storm-tossed ocean of time."

He broke for a few seconds to watch the waters, and then said,

"Think of it, your freshman year at the University of Florence! There's not a college in America that's a patch on the U. of Florence for general education. American colleges are parking lots, video arcades, nurseries."

"We're going to Italy?"

"We'll both be students. Your old dad's enrolling, too."

"In my classes? Say no."

"That would be fun, all right, but I won't have time for it."

"I see. New scheme?"

"Smart girl," he said. "We're looking to the future, right?"

From where I sat in Los Gatos, the future looked pretty bleak. I was ready to try anything. "I'll call Mom, see if she'll let me go."

He gave me one of those outrageous winks that make me envy de-Bobbed Mother. "I called her," he said. "She thinks it's a great idea. You'll spend the summer in Cleveland, then I'll swoop you up like a sudden wind. On September 15 sharp, we're off." One side of his face sagged. He said, "In confidence—save your money this summer. It's going to be a little tight."

"When hasn't it been?"

"True enough," he said. "That's how the world is made."

* * *

We set up in a miniapartment not far from Santa Croce. Actually, I got us the apartment. I'm the cautious kind, like my mother. To be ahead of the game, I spent my off-hours that summer nosing into Italian verbs and listening to E-Z Learn records. I didn't know much, but he knew nothing, so I was the one who talked to the agent, the lawyer, the landlord. Meanwhile Roberto, which he began calling himself the moment we touched Italian soil, waved his arms around and stretched his face. He had it in his head that Italians speak mostly with gestures, in a universal language without words, one human being to another. He pointed at things, stamped his feet, bugged out his eyes. By scaring the hell out of people, he most often got what he wanted.

I showed him where to sign the contract. He wrote his name
with a flourish: "Signor Roberto Bunsen." With considerable
style, then, he began laying out money. He had his pockets full of
cash. Four million lire he dropped on the table—ten months' rent
in advance.

"You didn't buy traveler's checks?" I said.

"That would have cost a percent, 180 bucks. We've got a better
use for the money."

"But what if you're mugged?"

"Out of a million people," he said, "how many get mugged? It's
a chance we'll take. Anyway, Italy's a civilized country, not like
America. Not everyone here is a criminal."

All the apartments in our building had triple locks. On the
streets, every first-floor window had a cage of iron bars driven into
the stone casing. When the shops closed for the evening, steel
shutters rumbled down, to be lock-bolted to pad eyes set in stone.
These features seemed more than just decorative. It seemed that
Florentine history had taught the citizens some lessons about human nature.

With his 180-dollar savings, and a lot more, he bought a new
suit, shoes, hat, briefcase, and typewriter. "There's an angle here,"
he said. "Business expenses are tax-deductible—we get it all back
from Uncle Sammy. You might call this trip free, kiddo."

"What business?"

"Glad you asked. I'm going to write a book." He paused to let
me apprehend the size of his ambition. "A book so new in concept
that, well, I might as well come right out with it—it's a cookbook.
I'm going to translate Tuscan cooking straight to the fair coasts
and valleys of California, and from that fertile market I'll expand
to all America."

"Dad, it's been done. There are maybe fifty Italian cookbooks
in English—you own three or four yourself."

"Have you heard of Boccaccio, kid? The *Decameron?* Ten people telling ten stories each, over a period of ten days? Well, they

tell these stories after lunch, which they call dinner because it's a big spread. So what did they eat, eh? Boccaccio forgot to mention it. I'm going to fill in the gap, kid. Ten complete lunches, from *antipasto* to *zabaglione*—fifty recipes, the most delicious Tuscan dishes. What do you think of my new suit? Like it?"

"Great idea, Dad—a kitchen companion to the *Decameron.* There must be, hell, ten or twenty people who would snap it up."

"Forget Boccaccio—he had his turn. This baby's all mine, stories, recipes, the whole thing. We go to restaurants, pick the best dishes, make notes. I take a cooking course at the school for foreigners. Meanwhile, I dream up the stories. Why won't you look at me, kid?"

"It's the suit," I said. It was of brown flannel, pin-striped in green and white, sharp-shouldered, nip-waisted, and with wide lapels and pleated trousers. "You're going to write a hundred stories?"

"It's a nice round number. We've got ten months. Hot tales, hot dishes—what do you think?"

"I think you oughtn't to be let loose in a men's store, for one thing."

"You watch," he said. "This suit will open doors. This suit is the key to the mint. We made the right move, kid. I can't remember when I felt so good. You hungry? Let's go find a trattoria. Let's get started."

* * *

We lived in Borgo Santa Croce, a dark street that seemed quarried out of solid rock. It ran northeast and southwest at an angle that, by my calculations, would let the sun in only once a year, at winter solstice, for about ten minutes in the afternoon. Our apartment was a converted attic, many flights of stone steps from the street. I slept on a camp cot by the dining table and kept my clothes in the china cupboard. Three steps from the table, the kitchen: a two-by-two gas range, tiny refrigerator, pan-sized sink.

Off the kitchen was what they called a *doccia integrale,* a toilet, basin, and shower all together. To take a shower, you had to remove the toilet paper and towels, then roll up one towel across the bottom of the door, for if water came out into the kitchen, it would sink between the tiles and, after a week's seepage in the stone walls, emerge in someone else's apartment. The first time I used it, my year's supply of Tampax swelled up and burst the box.

I don't want to enumerate only the inconveniences. I'm not so fastidious that I'll die if I sit on a germ. But I'm having a hard time thinking of amenities in our arrangement. Dad had the bedroom set up as a study, where he sat on the edge of the bed, using the nightstand as a typing table. He typed at his decameron. He typed recipes on cards and taped them in fine array on the walls. As a writer, though, he needed pacing room, and since he loved espresso, he was in and out of my part of the house like a steady stream of passersby.

I stayed away as much as possible. In the morning, I left while he was still asleep. On the way to class, I stopped at a bar for cappuccino and a sweet roll. After class, while the weather stayed nice, I went to the Boboli Gardens, over across the Arno, and sat sometimes in the pantheon, sometimes in one of the green grottoes, to do my homework. When the rains came in November, I moved into Santa Croce, the cathedral, and found a chapel with enough light to see by, and later, in the cold of winter, I went to the train station, ordered a pizza square and tea, and held possession of my little table for hours.

Whatever the weather, I came back home at six o'clock, to find him ending his first shift. Relative motion really gets to me. The thought that while I'm in one place, doing one thing, someone I care for is doing another thing somewhere else—well, for some reason it makes me feel like crying. At ten in the morning, say, when Professor Zappone asked me to conjugate the past-conditional mood of the verb "to be," it would occur to me that Dad was just then swinging his feet to the floor, shaking the fuzz from his head, trying to remember the story he was writing, while my mother, six time zones to the west, was getting into bed with substantial Eddie, probably cuddling to his back, submitting to, asking for, God knows what displays of affection.

The vastness of the space separating us would be suddenly in the room, would sweep around me, sweep me to the gaseous, intangible tip of the whirling galaxy. "I would have been, you would have been, he, she, it would have been, might have been . . ." Surrounded by the four solid walls of the classroom, with Professor Zappone's all too critical attention upon me, I would almost faint from sadness. How, out of Bob and Edie, could have come me? Two specks, endlessly awhirl, had chanced upon one another and spawned a third speck, now struggling in beginning Italian.

In my class, there were boys and young men of many kinds, Americans who seemed somehow damp, like new-hatched chicks, still sexless, and solemn Africans with long black fingers and, in their eyes, a wall with no opening to the inside. There were slim, arrogant Iranians and Israelis who hungered, other considerations aside, to fuck anything remotely female. Loud, smooth, blond German boys, one Swede as thin as a hacksaw blade, and an effeminate, small-featured Frenchman who, with reason, ran in fear of the black-eyed Iranians.

In the streets, Italian boys whistled and groaned, Italian men tried cutting me into corners, and Italian ancients, with lust like ashes in their faces, made courtly conversation. Sexually, I wasn't ready yet, nor in my heart and mind was I fit for love, but it wasn't only boys I shied from, for girls, too, seemed on the other side of their wants from where I stood. Their clothes, their laughter, the caprice in the way they walked and wore their hair: they were like butterflies dancing, mindless and beautiful, in the depths of a long perspective.

On Wednesdays I followed the Blue Guide to Florence but never got very far. I would start out, with unclouded intentions, for the Bargello, the Palazzo Vecchio, or the Uffizi Gallery, and on the way I would run into something, a church, say, or a monument, that would destroy me. Benvenuto Cellini's *Perseus,* in the loggia beside Piazza della Signoria: one day I glanced up into the demigod's implacable, drugged gaze, and I couldn't go on. He was looking right at me, offering the snake-infested head of Medusa. I froze there, my neck aching as I stared up, my feet sealed to the paving stones.

Another day, Blessed Alessio di Iacopo Strozzi finished me off, in Santa Maria Novella, as I was on my way to see Masaccio's *Christ Triumphant.* This saint, Blessed Alessio, according to the sign a Dominican and prior of the convent, lay fully dressed in a crystal coffin, his mouth open and wrenched sideways, nose gone, eye sockets empty now for exactly six hundred years. There was such tension in that mouth, straining to say one definitive word— what word was it, so long in coming?—that I turned and hustled out of there. I never went back to see the Masaccio.

I am not a good tourist. I can't pass through a church or museum, taking a casual look at things, and then move on to the next famous place on the list. No, I always see some one thing that knocks me out, that won't let me go on. I have never seen Michelangelo's *David* because, to get to it, you have to pass the *Captives,* those unfinished sculptures whose figures are still locked in stone. They can't get their arms, legs, or faces free from the marble blocks. I look at one of those trapped giants and I'm in a nightmare; I can't breathe; my legs are stuck; the fibers of my body entangle with the fibers of the rock mass around me. I sweat and gasp and embarrass myself. I pull myself away and run for the street.

Following the guidebook, one day, I came to a tiny piazza called Croce di Trebbio, where there was a fourteenth-century wooden cross of the Pisan school. A cross with no one nailed to it doesn't bother me much. But then I saw a note in the book. The scarred column on which the cross stood marks the spot where, in

A.D. 1244, there was a massacre of heretics. Five narrow streets enter that tiny space, there are high walls all around, and the heretics, jammed in there, trapped, were slaughtered with axes, spears, and clubs. Blood ran in the gutters, splashed the stone walls, and screams echoed after all those centuries, so that I had to clap my hands over my ears.

Not far away, in Piazza Santa Maria Novella, there's a plaque marking the spot where, in March of 1944, Jews were herded for shipment to Auschwitz, Buchenwald, and Mauthausen. That one paralyzed me, too. What was wrong with me? I kept getting stunned by things. I suppose I had no artistic taste. A dead pigeon in a puddle hit me as hard as Michelangelo's *Pietà*. Wherever I looked, X marked the spot where some horror had occurred. There were thousands of X's in the city.

The churches are graveyards, with people buried in the floors, the walls, the columns, in big boxes standing along the aisles, in the basements. Under the biggest church in town, the Duomo, there are graves from the former church, Santa Reparata, going back to Roman times. You hear strange noises down there, a humming, a kind of groaning, and something that sounds like organ music, muffled. Maybe it's the wind whipping, a hundred yards above the street, around the huge dome, or maybe it's the spirits of the dead, pressed under millions of tons of stone, howling out.

X marks Florence. Crucifixions, depositions, martyrdoms, death celebrated in churches and museums, while under the streets are layers of bones going back thousands of years. How could anyone be a historian, and actually study all that killing? It would freeze my heart. You don't find monuments to living things.

It didn't bother Dad at all. He got up at ten o'clock sharp, thinking of a story, thinking of lunch. He reviewed his recipes, adding a spice here and there, making notes, and whetting his appetite. He drank only water at that time of day, to keep his palate virginal. Then at one o'clock, he went to a restaurant or trattoria and worked through a five-course meal, his notebook open on the table. It took him a couple of hours. Back in the apartment, he would consolidate his notes before his taste buds forgot, and fall back for a nap. I came in at six, we went to dinner at eight, and then, when I'd gone to bed, he sat down to write the next installment of his decameron.

"This thing is getting really big," he told me. "I project it to around two thousand pages. A monumental work."

"You're getting kind of big yourself," I said. Under the forced feeding, he'd put on weight. The suit wouldn't button anymore and he'd stretched the underarm seams. Though he drank only an ordinary amount of wine with his meals, his face was as flushed as a drunkard's. "What do I do," I asked, "if you fall dead in the street here? You'd better leave some instructions."

He said, "Did you notice how they did that roast chicken tonight? They rubbed rosemary in between the skin and the meat—delicious."

"I'll throw up," I told him. "Let's not talk about dead meat."

"Well then, the veggies. Have you noticed how the Italians overcook them? Green vegetables should be cooked quickly, over a high flame, and then be served al dente, with a light sauce—butter, cream, or cheese."

"Should I have you shipped home, buried here, cremated? Have you made a will? How do I deal with the Italian bureaucracy, with a corpse on my hands?"

"The truth is," he said, "I think I've got a touch of gout. The knuckle of my right big toe has been killing me lately. It's caused by uric acid, crystallizing in the joint. The kidneys can't handle all the waste. We're living too high on the hog, kid, and that's the truth."

"How are we doing on money?"

"Not so hot," he said. "I've got a confession to make. That insurance policy, you know? Do you know about that?"

"You didn't," I said.

"Had to, kid. We'd pretty much gone through the eighteen thousand, what with the rent, your tuition, and so forth."

"I paid my own tuition, Dad. You ate, what, twelve thousand dollars in four months?"

"It's a tax write-off. We'll get it back."

"You cashed the insurance policy?"

"No, no—I wouldn't do a thing like that. Leave my daughter destitute? Roberto Bunsen? Never. I took out a little loan against it is all."

"How much did you borrow?"

"Not much—around thirty, I think it was."

"But the policy was only for forty thousand to begin with. In this decameron of yours, how many stories have you finished?"

"Hey now, did you ever try writing a hundred stories? It's a whole lot harder than I thought it would be. But I'm getting the hang of it, I'll really start whipping them out here."

"How many?"

"All completed? Checked for spelling, ready for the printer? Eight—but they're dandies, really nice stories, pretty sexy, some of them."

"Jesus, Dad."

"You know, kid, you're beginning to sound like your mother. I wouldn't go too far in that direction if I were you. It could lead to an unhappy life."

* * *

He had taken a one-month cooking course in October. In February he signed up for a real course, with heavy tuition, at one of Florence's famous restaurants. That's right, he handed over six thousand dollars and apprenticed himself to a chef named Trionfo Rigatelli, who put him to work in the kitchen for a good nine hours a day, with Mondays off. It was slave's work—stuffing pasta, chopping vegetables, sewing up the cavities of all sorts of carcasses before shoving them in the oven. He did a month of pastas, a month on meat, game, and poultry, a month on sauces, and a month on desserts. He got frantic with his notes. He was like a man trying to herd hummingbirds.

Meanwhile, I acquired a boyfriend. He came and sat beside me one day in a pew at Santa Croce. "May I show you this beautiful church?" he said. I said, "I've seen it, thanks. I'm reading. Go away." He said, "Ah, you speak Italian. You have a very good pronunciation. Are you English?"

"American," I said.

"That's even more remarkable. Americans, I often think, are born without lips, teeth, tongues. They mumble. They seldom master Italian, a language like fire in the mouth. It crackles, have you noticed? So crisp, so alive."

"How much to show me the church?"

"Shh," he said. "I'm not an approved guide—I'm not sanctioned. No money, therefore, must change hands. Of course, no one can prevent me from showing my church to a friend. Will you be my friend?"

"*Your* church?"

"I think of it as mine, yes. The priests think of it as theirs. The city fathers think they own it. It belongs to everyone—even to you, if you love it. Do you?"

"Not particularly. Too many tombs in here. I study here just to stay out of the cold."

"Tombs?" he said. "Why, these tombs are the only hope we have. They mark our progress in learning what it means to be human. There's Galileo over there—what a mind! There's Machiavelli, and along the wall, through there—Michelangelo! Gioacchino Rossini, too. Do you like music?"

"Okay, friend," I said. "Show me."

He was about seventy, and pretty creaky, but I hadn't realized he was nearly blind. From his raincoat pocket, he pulled a tattered guidebook, the cover heavily taped and with a sheaf of extra pages sewn in. Every page was black with notes, the margins filled, even the space between the lines filled in, with handwriting so tiny it looked like a smudge. He said, "First we must talk about"—he held the book right up against his eyes—"space!"

He shut the book and began telling me how, in the interior of a really fine church, the human spirit leaves the artificial confines of the body and expands to its true shape, rising above the corbels and joyfully rubbing its back against the high vaulting of the dome. "Notice," he said, "the shape that the spirit takes in Santa Croce. Look up, look all around you." He lifted his chin and moved his face back and forth, as if he'd caught a whiff of something good. "Notice," he said, "that the space is not symmetrical, that you're no longer in the logical dimension."

"If you don't earn money at this, how do you support yourself?"

"I'm retired," he said. "Now pay attention, child."

I paid attention for an hour, felt my spirit crawling precariously over the high capitals of the columns, in the groined vaulting of the smaller chapels, among the Gothic arches of the aisles, and up against the flat ceiling of the nave. I said, "Let's go have a glass of wine. Is that allowed?"

I led him to a bar just off Piazza Santa Croce, and for another hour he went on about space, taking me beyond the church and out into the universe. When he finished, he said, "Now we're ready to talk about Galileo. When will you come to the church again?"

"Tomorrow," I said.

"What's your name, child?"

"Stephanie—Stefania. What's yours?"

"Ermanno. Are we friends?"

"Sure, why not?" I said. "Tomorrow at three?"

I met him the next day, and, in front of Galileo's tomb, he spoke of the particular shape the spirit had taken in that man, whose eyes and mind reached out into our solar system. Along the way, we covered Copernicus and Kepler, dipped back to Pythagoras and Plato, then picked up Tycho Brahe on the way to Galileo again. He consulted his guidebook only twice, for dates, and as he talked he rubbed his fingers lightly on the stone facing of the tomb.

"This isn't a final resting place," he said. "This is a jumping-off place, a launchpad to the stars, so to speak. Renaissance, you know, means rebirth, and by doing homage to Galileo here, we remind ourselves that every day is a rebirth, that each morning, each one of us partakes of the general rebirth and is himself reborn. Or in your case, herself."

My love affair with Ermanno lasted for four months. In the chapels frescoed by Giotto, I learned how art crept from the cave of the dark ages, and at Michelangelo's tomb I followed art history into the bright noon sunlight. In the Pazzi Chapel, I had a course in the classical elements of Renaissance architecture, with Brunelleschi as prime example, and was urged to look at the Duomo again, with new eyes. He sent me to the Accademia di Belle Arti, the Bargello, the Duomo Museum, the New Sacristy at San Lorenzo—to see the sculptures of Donatello, Verrocchio, Giambologna, and Michelangelo. For a solid week, he spoke of the transfiguration of death through painting, and sent me to seek out Fra Angelico, Simone Martini, the Lippis, Cimabue, Giotto, Ghirlandaio. It wasn't God, he said, who put the lid on the Gothic style in Florence—it was the Florentines themselves. Witness Machiavelli, whose political thought so nearly conformed to the architectural shape of Santa Croce, in whose left wall he is buried.

Late in May, I said, "Dad, I want a thousand dollars." He said, "A thousand doll— kid, that's a lot of money."

"It would have been mine, anyway," I said. "I was the beneficiary. The divorce agreement between you and Mom—it's a legal document, isn't it? It specifically says you can't cash that policy or borrow against it. I'll blow the whistle on you."

"You will? You'll bite your father's hand, that feeds you? I tell you, I'm disappointed to hear that."

"Speaking of feeding, how could one man eat so many thousands of dollars' worth of food in so short a time?"

"Hey now, I'm not doing that anymore. I haven't got time, I don't even like food anymore. Look at me—I've lost weight. My toe feels good, I haven't had a Rolaid for weeks."

I had to admit he'd diminished some. The hideous suit almost fit him again. His face had been drained of the fireworks red color and, in fact, seemed a bit too pale, if anything. "I have to pay tuition," I said, "the final installment. For courses in history, art history, political science, science, philosophy, religion, the humanities."

"You're taking all those courses? I had no idea. No wonder I never see you."

I saw no reason to tell him who my teacher was. "Hand over the thousand," I said, "or I'll telephone Mom with the news."

The rest of the color left his face. From his jacket, he extracted a wad of money, counted out 1,400,000 lire. I said, "The exchange rate is fifteen hundred to the dollar."

"But when I bought this, it was only fourteen hundred," he said.

"That's what you get for not thinking. You lost one hundred lire per dollar on thirty thousand dollars. That's three million lire, or three-fourths of our whole ten months' rent."

"That much, eh?"

I kept my hand open. Grudgingly, he laid another hundred thousand on it.

But I couldn't find Ermanno. He stopped coming to Santa Croce, and I had no idea where he lived. By the first of June, the weather was getting hot, and I thought maybe he'd gone to the mountains or the sea. I asked one of the Franciscans, who move like brown ghosts in and out of the sacristy, for news. He misunderstood me. *"È morto Ermanno?"* he asked.

Was he dead? Could be. He was old enough to drop over at any time. Or, blind as he was, he could have been smashed by a car. The traffic is horrendous in Florence. On the off chance that he might be alive, I came to the church every afternoon, and began prowling the nearby streets, asking in the shops about a blind man, seventy or so, with arthritis in his hips and fingers.

Nothing. Couldn't find him. June went by. We had to leave.

The way we lived, getting out was harder than getting in. We had to ship boxes of Dad's notes and manuscripts, his typewriter, his new pasta machine, and a lot of culinary implements, and even then his briefcase and suitcases overflowed into mine with, among other things, the chef's hat, set personally on his head by Trionfo Rigatelli, as a mark of his having passed the cooking course.

The night before we left, we went to hear an organ concert at Santa Croce. As soon as we came in, I saw Ermanno in the back row of pews. I pulled Dad into the row and sat right next to him. "I missed you," I whispered. "Where have you been?"

"Stefania! How good to see you! I had to visit my mother for a few weeks, to help on the farm. She's getting a little feeble."

"Your mother? But how old is she?"

"Ninety-two. Shh, now—listen to Bach."

It was a program of preludes and fugues, toccatas, fantasias, and canzones. God, that organ! The basses rumbled in the huge space and the trebles flew around like birds. It was music like a sharp-prowed ship cutting through the sea, leaving behind a turbulent wake of sound. I held Ermanno's hand. He hummed one part or another of the broken music. He knew all the parts by heart.

Dad said, "Hey, what's going on? Who's the old guy?"

I whispered, "Shut up."

When it was over, I said, "Ermanno, we leave for America tomorrow. Thank you for everything."

"On the contrary, I thank you," he said. "You are a very nice young lady. The future rests with you."

"I love you," I said.

"And I love you. Never doubt it."

"Would you accept a gift?"

"If given with love, how could I refuse?"

It was only money, but I had nothing else. So I gave it to him, wrapped in a paper sack and held with a rubber band. "Take care of yourself, be well," I said. "Good-bye."

"Good-bye, Stefania," he said. We left. I said, "Dad, just don't open your mouth, all right?"

* * *

Well, we flew home. Dad to San Francisco, I to Detroit. I took the Greyhound to Cleveland and spent the summer with Edie and Eddie, working at the dry cleaner's, saving my money. On September 1, I flew to California, moved into my old bedroom, and enrolled at Bay State University, where I study finance.

Dad's book, miracle of miracles, got published. It has eight stories, with recipes for eight long lunches, and the stories, though not pornographic, are nasty enough to attract the kind of people who would eat five courses at noon. So he's making a pile of money. He's a hot item on the speakers' circuit and TV talk shows. He quit teaching history, of course, and is now putting together his second book, "Evenings with Roberto"—in which he tells stories in his own voice, serves the food, and selects one of the female guests for special attention after the fruit and cheese. This one's really disgusting, but his publisher offered him a whopping advance on it.

As for me, I'm in a holding pattern. I need a few more years, not many, before going back to Florence. It's not maturity I lack —it's time. You see, in a burst of generosity, Dad gave me the entire forty thousand dollars from the insurance policy. "It's the least I could do," he said. "Why should you wait till I die? Take the money and run. Buy some baubles."

I ran to a broker and bought stocks. I go for growth. I've got to parlay this once-in-a-lifetime thing into a future. In a couple of years, if my luck holds, I'll be able to take a conservative position and live for a while on dividends.

I know all too well the genetic discrepancies between my father and mother. But education can work wonders. I hope to turn my defects into triumphs. I'll start by finding Ermanno, to learn about music, and then I think I'll study history, big history, from the primordial bang, the Word, to wherever time takes me. I don't know how it'll end, I wouldn't make any bets, but if you see an unusually bright fireball streaking through the sky some night, it might be me.